Save a Prayer Sunset

Save a Prayer Sunset

LANCE GARRISON

TATE PUBLISHING
AND ENTERPRISES, LLC

Published by Tate Publishing & Enterprises, LLC
127 E. Trade Center Terrace | Mustang, Oklahoma 73064 USA
1.888.361.9473 | www.tatepublishing.com

Tate Publishing is committed to excellence in the publishing industry. The company reflects the philosophy established by the founders, based on Psalm 68:11,
"The Lord gave the word and great was the company of those who published it."

Book design copyright © 2016 by Tate Publishing, LLC. All rights reserved.
Cover design by Samson Lim
Interior design by Jomar Ouano

Published in the United States of America

ISBN: 978-1-68270-914-6
1. Fiction / Christian / Suspense
2. Fiction / Christian / General
16.02.12

ACKNOWLEDGMENT

To my Lord and Savior, Christ Jesus, thank you for saving me and washing me clean in your blood. Amen.

Now to my sons, Tylor and Preston—may the Lord's blessings shine down upon you both with Holy grace and mercy from above. I love you both dearly.

An extended thank you also goes to Kerri Gray for being one of my dearest friends when most had given up on me. Same for Paula McHenry, for never giving up on me and always checking in, either by phone or by letter, to give encouragement in my new-found walk with Christ Jesus. Thank you both, and God Bless.

And to David Altom for your gifted genius in all things computers. If not for you, there never would have been a book. Literarily. Also to Cindy Altom—thanks for your kindness.

Also, warmest thanks to my parents. You put up with more than you should.

Last, but certainly not least—a heartfelt thank-you to, Mr. Morgan Freeman. Your time spent on *The Electric Company* helped me learn to read. Don't ever think for a moment Mr. Freeman that your talent during that period in the seventies was wasted. It wasn't. God Bless you as well, Morgan Freeman.

1

These soft, low-grumbling murmurs encapsulated the board meeting at International Creative Management and swarmed around Derek Harris and began to choke his every thought as if an unforeseeable force laid hold tight to the words lodged deep within the delicate framework of his heated mind and would not relinquish its grasp for any coherent utterance to pass from his lips.

He was at a cerebral standstill and couldn't get it together enough to rectify the production problem that had just been pitched at his feet. All he wanted was out from where he sat. He felt if he stayed where he was any longer, he might lash out at the nearest associate.

A room full of them. Eight to be exact. Always a clean, even number when million-dollar-budget-decisions were at stake.

Like the one now, before Derek.

His mind finally gave way to some form of clarity and everything became tranquil and serene.

Derek Harris was back.

Out of his seat, he was in the middle of the conference room—in charge—once more—like always.

"Look," he finally said, "everyone relax. Attacking the problem this way, won't fix it." His attention swiftly turned to Susan, a cosmetically enhanced beauty. "Now, what's the hold up?"

Soft blue eyes stared out from behind wisps of blonde bangs and up from the spread sheet. "Lions Gate," Susan said, "doesn't want to shell out Chaz Spivey's asking price anymore."

"Get me Marty Shaw on the line."

Shaw was Lions Gate's CEO and main go-to whenever problems arose. Which always did. Problems and movie making are inseparable. They go together, like rain to mud. If Derek didn't find a way quick to resolve the issue at hand, *he'd* be rung through the mud, so to speak.

From the speaker phone, the voice of Lions Gate's CEO filled the conference room.

Shaw: I know why you called, Derek. But answer's no. Lions Gate will not pay, Chaz Spivey's asking price. It's just too high.

Derek: That wasn't your opinion last year.

Shaw: That was last year.

Derek: But Wine and Roses screams Oscar.

Shaw: Chaz Spivey isn't the only A-lister we can get. Think you're the only agent in town who handles talent the American-movie-going public craves? Half your roster Derek is slammed with overly pampered, self-indulgent actors who think they're actually worth more than what they get. Worth more than a twenty-million dollar payday. I swear.

Derek: Then swear you'll do this Marty. Even if it go against your best judgment.

Shaw: Nothing's inked yet, so no. No, I won't swear. Sorry.

Derek: We go way back, Marty.

Shaw: This won't end our working relationship.

Derek: It could mine with Chaz Spivey.

Shaw: Then convince him his price is way out of hand.

Derek: If his price goes down is he in?

Shaw: You know once an actor gets a taste of the extravagant, there's no hope.

Derek: If his price goes down?

Shaw: Okay…If his price goes down.

Derek: Say it, Marty. I want to hear you say it.

Shaw: If Chaz Spivey comes down on his price than maybe we can go into further discuss. But I mean way down. Not just a couple hundred grand either, Derek.

You're his agent. Talk to him. Like how you smoke-screened him into believing he's really worth, twenty-million a picture.

A dial tone echoed. The conversation was snuffed.

When Shaw was done, he was done. Typical Hollywood edict. Of course, it could have and maybe should have gone much worse. Which Derek knew. Which made him grateful. There was an off-handed chance to try and wrangle Chaz Spivey away from another twenty-million dollar payday. Derek had his work cut out for him.

He turned from the speaker phone. Blank faces were before him. No need for any in-depth explanation because the entire conference room had heard, from Shaw himself, what had to be done. And quick.

"Let's call it a day," Derek said. "Tomorrow will be here soon enough." He watched the room of ICM's finest empty out.

Todd Allen; then Mark Rosenberg; then Gabe Rhodes; then Jeff Rossdale; then Mike Childress; then Brent Harrington; then Nathan Porter.

All agents, except Susan. Her duties were strictly secretarial.

She was at the door. Her well-manicured hand kept it slightly ajar.

"Anything else, Mr. Harris?" Susan always covered bases. Dependable and never late. Susan had been Derek's secretary, twelve years running, ever since he became an ICM agent—straight out of law school. Derek couldn't imagine anyone else doing what Susan did. She definitely made Derek's workload less stringent.

"No, Susan…Go ahead and go."

The door closed behind her.

Now it was just Derek—there—alone—in the conference room. No one to step-up and have his back on this one.

He glanced at the wall and eyed the clock.

"I'm late," he whispered, and thought of home.

His family waited.

2

"**D**addy!"

Precious, little Jessica. Lucky to have perfect sight.

In her crib one night, few weeks after taking her first new steps as an infant—and after Derek had rocked her to sleep and laid her down—Jessica woke, rolled over, hoisted herself up, managed to get one chubby leg over that wooden railing of her crib, balanced herself for a few brief seconds before shifting her weight too far to the left, and toppled, head-first to the floor below—array of toys scattered about.

And it was that array of toys scattered about—plastic dump truck on its side that had sent Jessica whaling in a fit of bloodstain pain—straight to the emergency room—for five carefully placed stitches above her left eye.

All Jessica had to show for the mishap, which she remembered not—was a slight, pinkish scar. That, and perfect sight. Such subtle ways, grace abounds.

Derek picked her up, tight to hip. "How's my girl, huh? School go good today?"

Jessica was six and a half and in her second semester of first grade—straight A's and holding tight. A near-perfect 4.0. Not bad for a first grader.

"Guess what," she said.

Derek grinned. "What?"

"You're a monkey." Jessica flashed her missing-front-tooth smile. "And I'm not." She wiggled free from Derek's hip and hid behind the sofa. "You can't find me."

This was the usual game played when Derek got home. Not that he minded. Every time he saw Jessica and that slight, pinkish scar above her left eye—memories of five emergency room stitches—flooded back. A memory forever etched in Derek's mind. So, the cute game played was fair trade.

He couldn't help but grin. "Jess, I just saw you high-tail it behind the sofa. How could I not know where you're at?" Derek loved the game, too; only in loving ways Jessica had yet to comprehend, but sensed—sensed that protective, caring nature Derek, her daddy enveloped around her—his precious, little Jessica.

On hands and knees, Derek stalked closer to the far-end of the sofa. "I'm getting closer, Jess…Closer, still, I am."

"So, what!" Jessica pounced. "You're a monkey." She flashed her missing-front-tooth smile again and landed on Derek's back. "Now, you're a donkey."

"Jerk is more like it. You're late again. Why?"

The cute game was over.

Jessica still hugged-tight to his back, Derek got to his feet. "Hey, hon." Jessica slid down and sat on the sofa.

Derek made his move. He tried to caress a kiss on his wife's cheek.

Amber would have none it. Not now.

Eight weeks and going strong, Derek's arrival home had been delayed and put off for some misplaced reason, or other. Chill-laden fears of an affair of the heart with another woman, now lately, gripped Amber. And she had every right to such fears—as would any wife.

"I'm sorry," Derek said. Still, the apology came off, not quite so sincere. There was this odd, blank gaze to his eyes, as if something else held his silent attention. Derek just couldn't shake the thought of Chaz Spivey not landing the lead role in *Wine and Roses*.

Tears swelled. "Go to your room, sweetie," Amber told Jessica.

"You and Daddy fighting again?" Jessica knew something was amiss. She had seen, on more than one occasion, not just tonight, Derek and Amber—cold and distant to each other—as ice to skin.

Derek tried to be as assuring as he could. "No-no, Jess… I'm just tired and Mommy's just—"

Choice words filled the air. Amber had never spoken such language in front of Jessica. But Derek's constant, inconsiderate disregard for not being home on time, had pushed Amber past her limit. Eight weeks of this was enough. More than enough. Amber wanted a solid answer. Not just sorry, anymore.

To hear anger in her mommy's voice like that, caused tears to swell, too. But unlike Amber, Jessica could not contain the raw emotion that suddenly churned the very pit of her stomach.

She ran for her room in a fit of hysterics—slammed her bedroom door shut and locked it. Then the tears Jessica fought so hard to contain, flowed in heated streaks down her flushed cheeks like tiny, hot translucent pearls.

"See what you did to her," Amber cried.

"Me…? You came in and threw a fit."

"Because you're late again." The dreaded question that ate at Amber finally blurted out. "Are you seeing someone, Derek? Just tell me."

"What?"

"You're never here."

"What do you mean, never here?" Derek knew exactly what Amber meant. But how could he tell the woman he loved and mother of his child, that life and that ever slow-present, work-related grind was closing in—set to get the best of him.

So much so, Derek had been tempted in weeks past to seek some form of professional help. Instead, after-work drives on the 101 freeway was the closet he got in seeking professional help. And because so, he was where he was—in his house, in front of Amber, Jessica in her room now crying—and Derek sadly left to try and wrap everything up in a way that Amber would finally understand and come to accept.

"Oh, you're here," she said. "But not *really* here." That dreaded question blurted out again. "Are you seeing someone, Derek? The truth. That's all I want. Just the truth."

"No."

Faith placed in Derek's answer wasn't so easy for Amber to do because she still had doubts of heavy lingering suspicion. "I want to know where you've been."

"In a meeting," Derek said. "It ran longer than expected. I'm probably going to lose Chaz Spivey as client. Lions Gate won't—"

"I'm not talking just about tonight, Derek. For two months, it's been the same with you. Late. Always late. Always something. I'm sick of it. Of the whole thing." Amber's tear-stained eyes scanned the spacious living room. Best money could buy. All there in the house in Bel-Air. Derek had owned up to his role as provider.

In terms of materialism, Amber couldn't complain. She had everything she ever wanted: four cars in a four car garage; maid, three days a week; hair and nails done, Beverly Hills style whenever the urge arose; credit cards, thirty grand limit each; trendy Cheesecake Factory meals; and Rodeo Drive shopping sprees on whim. Long and winding list of perks for Amber. And she knew it. She also knew—"Our marriage is falling apart." Her tear-stained eyes locked hard onto Derek. "Can't you see that? Can't you see where all this is headed?"

How could he not? His marriage was slipping away faster than the last reel of an overly melodramatic movie, where he was hero and villain, all rolled into one. A heartfelt change had to be made. More than just "sorry" would be required—more than just a minor adjustment, here and there. What faced Derek head on was an entire life revision at the root foundation he had built his life upon. Total stock had to be tallied and an internal audit done. Clean house in other words was in due order.

But first, Derek had to take that first fearful step forward and confess to Amber, his real reason why he had been so late, each night—eight weeks straight coming home.

"This is hard to say but—"

"You want a divorce," Amber said. "I knew it." She also knew how she longed to be touched.

Derek got the silent message. He took her hand. "No," he said. "I don't want a divorce."

"Then what is it?"

"I think I'm having a mental breakdown…Or something. Things just don't seem right, anymore. I'm losing focus at work. And—"

"Here at home, too." Amber's hand slipped away from Derek's gentle grip. Then the jolting implication finally registered. "What do you mean, a mental breakdown?" Amber was back holding Derek's hand.

"Just like I said, a mental breakdown. I think I'm about to have one."

"That's silly." Amber was in no way ready to face the possible truth that her husband of twelve years was losing his grip on sanity and slowly spiraling off into the abyss of fragile madness. Because if so—if Derek, indeed, fell prey to mental disarray—nothing again would ever be the same. Not for Amber; not for Jessica—and certainly not for Derek.

"Really," he said. "Is it really that silly, Amber?"

She knew it wasn't but didn't want to accept it. "That's not what I meant," she said. "But you, Derek? You're just not the type to have one of those."

"A mental breakdown?"

"Stop saying that."

"Don't know what else it could be."

"Lots of things. But not a mental breakdown. Not one of those." Amber quickly shifted subjects. "Now, what's this about you maybe losing Chaz Spivey as client?"

"Amber, c'mon."

"Really," she said. "I want to know." Derek's late night homecomings didn't seem such an inconvenience anymore—nor something to be explained away. Not if it meant having to hone up to the truth of what lay ahead.

"Thought you wanted to know why—"

"Because work's been hectic, right? I mean you may very well lose your most valuable client."

"And my mind."

"Enough, Derek. No more talk about that."

"But that's why I've been home, late here, for weeks past. Things have been closing in around me, so much. Not just at work, either. That the only thing I could think to do was drive the 101…For hours."

At least it's not another woman, Amber thought. Divorce papers no longer pranced in her head. For a moment, she thought she might be the guilty cause in all this—all Derek was going through? Fast track back, and Amber traced the weeks prior in her mind—the weeks Derek came home late each night.

Nothing registered. She couldn't think of anything she might have done to cause Derek to act the way he did. Still, she had to ask—"Have I done anything, Derek? Did I—"

"No, Amber. You haven't done anything." Derek's gaze fell to the floor. "Tell you honest, though, I really think it's work. The pressure. You wouldn't believe. You just wouldn't." His gaze returned to Amber. "It's getting harder and harder to keep pace." It was true. The average life expectancy for an ICM agent was ten years, tops. And Derek had very well eclipsed that average, twenty-four months ago. He was freefalling steadily into agent burn out.

"And if I lose Chaz Spivey as client…Well…"

Amber knew good and well, what "well" meant. "If you do," she said, "there'll be some up-and-comer to take his place." Spot on. There was always some fresh, new twenty-something to garnish and secure agent representation. "Remember how you met, Chaz? At that Industry party."

Actually, it was a showcase in the valley, set up by Chaz Spivey's high school teacher, Mr. McNaire (he had known Derek through a friend of a friend who had known Mr. McNaire)—and felt Chaz had more talent to spare then most his age and would be a viable asset to an ICM agent like, Derek Harris.

"Yeah," he said. "I remember."

Neither Amber nor Derek had noticed Jessica—after calming down and tears dry and Little Mermaid jammies on—unlock her bedroom door, sneak down the hall, pass the bathroom and kitchen, and crawl behind the sofa again—listening in now on all being said. Well, almost all. Jessica had only been behind the sofa, roughly less than five minutes. But enough to get the gist.

Her squeaky sneeze gave away her whereabouts. That, and those white Little Mermaid plastic footies, poking out behind the sofa.

"We got a spy," Derek said. "Sure enough, a spy." He also had tear-filled eyes now, and didn't want to know what else lay ahead of him, either. The day's meeting had been more than enough, and there was still Chaz Spivey to deal with.

Amber was at the edge of the sofa. "And a cute spy, too." She grabbed Jessica's Little Mermaid footie.

"Aw," she said, playful squirm, "you found me, Mommy. No fair."

"Plenty fair," Derek said, eyes clear and bright now. "Especially when it's passed your bedtime, sweetie." He held Jessica in his arms. "Off we go, we do. Back to bed, we do."

Jessica pinched his nose. "Daddy?"

"Yes," he said, casting a quick glance at Amber—hand over heart. She was always touched to see how Derek cared for and pampered, Jessica. She still had his nose in a pinch.

"Everything'll be fine…Monkey."

"There's nothing wrong, Jess," Amber chimed in.

"Everything'll be fine," she said again and gently laid her head upon Derek's shoulder, eyes fluttering shut. Jessica was gone. Deep sleep.

"Don't worry," Derek told Amber. "I'll get her to bed."

Suddenly, Jessica's head rose. "The man in my room said so."

"What man?" Derek feared. So did, Amber.

"Well," Jessica yawned, "he's really an angel, he said." Jessica laid her head down upon Derek's shoulder again. And she was gone again. Deep sleep again.

"You know," Amber said, "Jess made that up because she knows there's something going on between us, Derek. Children sometimes do that because of fights in the family. They sometimes make up an imaginary friend."

Derek smiled. "Like an angel?" He felt Jessica's tiny, rhythmic breathing against his chest.

"Yes," Amber said, "like an angel."

"What better friend to have, than an angel," Derek grinned. He then told Amber, "Go ahead and go to bed. I'll put Jess down."

"She already is," Amber whispered. "But go ahead."

Derek made his way quietly to Jessica's room, then to her bed, then pulled back the sheets, gently laid her down, and kissed her forehead, near that slight, pinkish scar above her left eye.

"Goodnight, Jess. Daddy loves you."

At her bedroom door, Derek turned and was thankful that Jessica now slept in a full-size bed—never again to be laid down in a crib, where she could fall, head first—to the floor below.

The door slowly closed.

Now all Derek had on his mind was Chaz Spivey and how to approach him with the news of his commission price. After that—would be the nagging mental disarray that still lingered.

Down the hall, Derek whispered—"An angel. Can you believe that?"

His thoughts soon latched back onto Chaz Spivey.

3

12:32 a.m.

Polaroid pictures were strewn about like haphazard puzzle pieces. Each photo had captured a celluloid segment of Chaz Spivey's lazy, carefree high school days before being discovered and pluck from absolute obscurity by Derek Harris—top-brass ICM agent and gatekeeper to all that Hollywood offered.

Once signed as client and head-shot ready, after graduation and diploma in hand, Chaz Spivey hit audition after audition. And landed audition after audition. Commercials first, then guest roles, here and there— *90210, Melrose Place, Law & Order*—even a few character driven spots on whatever hip series HBO or Showtime had carefully crafted.

Which eventually lead Chaz Spivey down the multi-million dollar path of bona-fide, trend-setting movie star and became infamously known as "the face" of American cinema. Such accolades as these—all in the span of less than five years, since meeting Derek Harris—fourteen-some-odd years back.

Or was it fifteen, Chaz guessed. His eyes still honed in on the worn and faded Polaroids of long ago. Yesteryears cried out to be relived. If only for a moment. If only Chaz could. But he couldn't it—and knew it.

Still, that didn't stop desire from rising high and choking out sound reason.

Get back to films that cater to the youth. Forget all this silly romance junk. Leave all that to John Cusack.

Hazel eyes turned away from the Polaroids, and the song, *Pictures of You*, by *The Cure*, drummed silently within Chaz Spivey's head, and wouldn't relent until he was in the bathroom.

He now stood before the mirror.

It teased.

Eighteen had long since passed.

Age, that stealthily robber of youth was creeping up, ever-so-ready to wither, Chaz Spivey—day by day, minute by minute—to where he really didn't know why he was even still an actor. Movie after movie no longer held ego-thrills of self-righteous importance.

In fact, nothing did anymore. Not like how it once did—fourteen-some-odd years ago. Or was it fifteen?

The mirror still teased.

And that painful, reflective glare, pierced deep—Chaz Spivey's conceited self-worth.

Enough of this. If I want to feel bad, I'll read the trades.

But he didn't want to read the trades.

A sudden jolt of memory-lane-days, drove Chaz Spivey—straight to the closet.

He began to rummage.

There.

Found.

In the closet.

The box.

The same box that had been packed away after fame hit; and the same cardboard box that hid—at the very bottom, under stale, yellowed tax returns, and who know what else—a near forgotten address book.

Hazel eyes honed in.

The address book was opened.

Sprinkled throughout were names and numbers Chaz hadn't seen since his teenage days. All girls, they were, when Chaz was only sixteen, back then, and still in high school—not thirty-plus, like now.

Quickly, he dialed off the first number. No luck. In fact, every attempt to reach the other girls, by number, that had been inked down in that once lost address book— proved futile.

But then there was the last page.

Only one name remained: Heather Stockton, number, 213-555-8956, smudged so faint from passing years, Chaz could hardly make it out. He tore the page from the address book and held it up against the light. Heather's number could clearly been seen now.

Cell phone got, Chaz dialed the number.

Call roamed.

Be there, c'mon.

Chaz didn't know why he was doing this other than Heather Stockton had been a rather late-teen crush, and rather serious one, too. Only Chaz had kept that little tidbit to himself.

I should've told her when I had the chance.

Finally—"Hello?" It was a groggy female voice.

"Heather?" Chaz almost sounded childlike again—as if no time had passed and still sixteen.

The groggy female voice became stout. "Who is this?"

The question cut sharp and deep because Chaz Spivey had grown weary of hiding behind his false manufactured Hollywood persona—that no longer could he stand the lie he lived in—even if that lie afforded him a life spoiled in privileged luxury amongst the flippant movers and shakers of profane excess whose vast wealth kept them securely grounded within the financial boardwalk of America's top 2 percent.

"Who is this?" said the groggy female voice again.

No hesitation this time. "Cody Holt." Chaz Spivey had finally come clean—to none other than a complete stranger, by phone—and said his birth given name, before Hollywood changed it.

"It's past one in the morning."

"I know, Mrs. Stockton." Cody then gave his reason for his inconsiderate inquiry; that he had found Heather's number, and thought, she might be home, where she grew up. After all, the Thanksgiving holiday was near—ten days near.

"No, Heather's not here. She lives in New Mexico now." Mrs. Stockton shouldn't have but added, "Hobbs."

"Is she married?"

"None of your business."

The call was swiftly dropped.

After all, had Mrs. Stockton really known who she was talking to, whether Heather was married, or not, might have been drawn out for further, in-depth discussion. Even at such a late hour.

"Heather's not married," Cody convinced himself. "If she were, Mrs. Stockton would've said so. I need a map. Maybe there, in the closet?"

Sure enough.

On the top shelve, under a stack of old, dated scripts which had helped Cody Holt seal his now infamous image as Chaz Spivey—was a map—old and more so dated than the stack of scripts, it seemed. The map felt like brittle, sun baked leaves—than once bright and clean paper. But it would do.

Hazel eyes fell upon, The Land of Enchantment, and spied Hobbs, New Mexico.

It's at the very bottom of the state. How did Heather ever end up there?

The notion to go and find her came sudden. Wasn't as if Cody had a normal job to cover and ask, time off. No worry over money, either. He was far beyond set for life in that department. Cody Holt's bank account was well-balanced and stable—never to tip passed the overdrawn scales. Sixty-million-plus has that safety-net assurance.

I'll just go and find her. And if she is married…I'll run.

Cody Holt/Chaz Spivey couldn't stand being around guys. Even in his formative years, if a testosterone fueled group of muscle bound jocks was in the hall at school, or carousing around town, Cody would heel-toe quick—the opposite way. No fanfare; and under no way, whatsoever, any eye contact. Nothing ensures a sure-fire beat down on a polite and rather feminine looking teenage boy, than eye contact made in the general direction of a testosterone fueled group of muscle bound jocks.

But that had been ages ago.

Not how it was now for, Cody Holt—metaphorically incognito as, Chaz Spivey. No sure-fire beat down, anymore. Not since bodyguard protection had been so handsomely bought—in crisp, clean hundred dollar bill denomination. That, and the state-of-the-art security system—personalized in special, private code, to alert—the Beverly Hills P.D.

I really should sell this place.

It had gotten way too distant for just one person alone. Sure, Cody had molded himself near-perfect, in terms of aesthetic seduction to the female population. Still, that hadn't secured true love. That most sought after emotional commodity, stayed far, wide and away. Love was the one thing that fame, nor money—sixty-million-plus—could never truly snare. Not even for Cody Holt/Chaz Spivey— by himself, all alone in a much too massive home.

At the closet again, about to place the cardboard box back inside—just below the top shelve, Cody noticed a bible—a New American Standard bible. Its leather bound cover still held a deep, worn crease down the middle.

The Holy Bible was quickly opened.

Hazel eyes spied the hand-written inscription. It read: Cody, I'm so thrilled to see how God, the Father has blessed you with such awe-inspiring talent. So, as you enter the world of "new" graduates, please remember to use those blessed talents to bring forth glory to our Lord and Savior, Christ Jesus. Sincerely, Mitch Taylor.

My old youth pastor. Cody quivered.

Sheer terror soon gripped—because those awe-inspiring talents had not once been used to bring forth glory to the Lord and Savior, Christ Jesus. All glory, fame and money had been laid before Cody's unworthy feet—solely through the brazened image of Chaz Spivey—silver-screen-day-dream-fantasy and midnight sex symbol to hordes of overly zealous female fans.

A far-distant, sinful memory, years back—suddenly surfaced.

Cody relieved that horror-filled night again—the discord—the anger—the resentment. A raging temper tantrum had gotten the very best of Cody Holt—while, under the intoxicate influence of heavy drink and psychedelic drugs.

That unsavory mixture in cocktail had warped and lowered Cody's inhibitions, down below, "less than zero." He hadn't really wanted to say what he did. But he did, and had straight-up, cursed God, that night with such cruel, insulting slang—had anyone heard—would have trembled in fear of eternal damnation.

By now, the memory kept replaying without relenting relief.

Cody didn't know what to do.

He frantically flipped the pages of the bible—in search of the one gospel that would either bring divine spiritual hope or lose of eternal redemption.

Hazel eyes fell upon the book of Matthew—twelfth chapter—thirty-second verse.

The warning of Christ Jesus ministered: And whoever shall speak a word against the Son of Man, it shall be forgiven him; but whoever shall speak against the Holy Spirit, it shall not be forgiven him, either in this age or the age to come.

That memory of long ago, of heinously cursing God— surfaced again, and tore deep inside, Cody Holt.

He whispered—"I think I may have committed the unpardonable sin. I think I may have blasphemed, the Holy Spirit."

Cody Holt shuddered.

4

Years of senseless bloodshed and inhuman acts of violence upon women, children, and the elderly had just about numbed over Curtis Paxton's conscience. Everyday seemed like another day of the exact same: random shootings, countless rapes, back-alley prostitution, mob shakedowns, and the worst to stomach—child abductions.

Sure, other crimes were morally grotesque, in their own right, but there was something so nefarious about a case that involved a missing child because violent crimes were usually, not always, but most times—played out upon those little helpless ones that were so innocent to the vile, evil of this present world.

This is what Curtis had to deal with every working day—every moment he was clocked in as detective, Paxton—there, upon the streets of Los Angeles—the City of Angels. But angels, at least the heavenly kind it seemed, were in short supply.

"Time of death," he asked a CSI investigator, and looked up from the female body. Rigor mortis had already set firm and hard upon her once alive and beautiful face—now pallor pale with dull, lifeless eyes—locked in a blank stare, off in the ether—where eternal space and time stretch forth passed the light fantastic. Just another case to be filed under, senseless bloodshed and inhuman acts of violence.

"Probably close to…Oh, I'd say, two this morning." The CSI investigator rose from bent knee. "Won't really know from sure though until we get her downtown."

The body bag was zipped up and placed in the back of a waiting ambulance. No time sooner, either.

A crowd of on-lookers had suddenly appeared. Something Paxton, by now, had gotten use to but hated, just the same. Death always draws a morbid crowd.

"Well," he said, "do just that. Get her downtown." He slapped the back of the ambulance. "Don't give the death tourists here anymore reason to stick around."

He watched the ambulance round the corner of the street, out of sight. He wondered when his time would come and when he would be pronounced dead and placed in the back of a waiting ambulance? But unlike most victims logged in downtown and ushered off to the coroner, after death had come ever so sudden and quick—Paxton had family and was loved. Especially by wife, Amanda.

Remembrance of their wedding—fifteen-years ago—on a slightly over-cast day, gentle rain upon crisp, autumn leaves in late November was a subtle reminder that Mr. and Mrs. Paxton's anniversary wasn't but a few days away.

Paxton took mental note of the gift, a pair of diamond earrings, he would later buy at Zales. He then turned to the voice that resonated from behind. Ryan Garrett had finally arrived on the scene.

"What do we got?"

"We had a murder," Paxton announced, "until the ambulance sped off with the victim." He stared hard at Garrett. "Where were you?"

"Had a rough night," he grinned. "Sorry."

"No, you'll be sorry if Captain Spurgin finds out. Don't let this happen again." Paxton didn't let on but understood because he too had once been the young Turk on the beat— and had, his first few months on the streets—turned up late to an investigation.

"I won't. Promise."

"Don't make promises you can't keep." Paxton addressed an on-duty policeman. "Me and my partner here'll be across the street." He guided Garrett to a diner/coffee shop.

They took a seat in the back.

As if on cue, a middle aged waitress was at the table. Her face—make-up, overload; eyes, lined heavy in black liner; lips, painted almost clownish red; neck, sun damaged, hands as well—showed just how desperate she was to preserve what was left of her fading youth.

Years ago, Nancy Cox had been a drama darling with talent in spades in character development and voice. But like how it goes for so many who travel the beaten path of actor and hop bus to Hollywood—only disappointment had embraced, Nancy Cox. Nothing fell in her favor. Acceptance-speech-daydreams were relegated to a lonely, smoke-filled diner/coffee shop—downtown, Los Angeles.

"The same, Curtis?" Nancy knew Paxton. He had been a regular for two years. "Coffee, full stack, side of bacon?" He nodded. Nancy scribbled down the order and turned to Garrett. "And you, Crocket?"

Garrett grinned at the *Miami Vice* reference. "The same."

Two cups of coffee were poured and Nancy walked off and placed the request with the short order cook behind the counter. He got busy, grilling away at Paxton and Garrett's late breakfast.

Anticipation got the best of Garrett. "Are we really here for breakfast?"

"We need to talk," was Paxton's subtle reply.

"About?"

"Your tardy stunt this morning."

Garrett glanced out the window. "I said it wouldn't happen again." His gaze returned to Paxton. "Promise. Like I said."

Paxton toyed at his coffee with a tarnished spoon, trails of white steam rising. "It's not just you being tardy." He put the spoon down. "There's more."

"Well, I can assure you I also changed my underwear this morning, encase you're wondering."

Paxton grinned; then got serious. "It's the crimes you'll be around. Sooner or later, they'll get to you." He now knew the talk was more for him than Garrett.

"Have they you?"

"Some." Paxton wished he hadn't honed up to that because if Garrett were to place a report, Paxton could very well be brought up for psychological evaluation, and if found unstable for duty, be placed on permanent sabbatical until found mentally sound again. "But I hope this just stays between us."

"Same with my tardy stunt this morning."

"Agreed." Paxton watched Nancy finally make her sudden return. Smell of hot cakes and bacon, overwhelmed.

Paxton and Garrett didn't know how hungry they were until their order was before them. They said, "Thanks," in unison.

A splash of coffee re-fills. "You're welcome," Nancy said, and walked off, order pad in apron pocket, pen behind ear, to another table—way in front.

The first bite of late breakfast satisfied. Paxton and Garrett savored each fork full—quick coffee-wash-down. Half done, the conversation resumed.

"So," Garrett said, "just what should I expect out there on the streets?" This was his freshman year as Detective—and would discover soon enough—just how much unabashed human horror awaited him on the streets there in Los Angeles.

Last sip of coffee finished off, Paxton recounted the one case that still haunted him…

———

Few steps behind, upon exiting the Yellowbird school bus, Melissa Sanders lost sync with fellow classmates. Not that she really cared. More was on her mind than trashy, ninth grade gossip because Melissa was four days late.

Pregnancy hadn't been something on the agenda or radar—neither had falling hard for senior star quarterback and college bound, Matt Miller. Teenage hormones always seem to over-ride any logic in sound reason—especially when such teenage hormones are so heavily intertwined around the heart.

And Melissa Sanders had been no different than any other girl her age when it came teenage hormones because she became weak and had caved in during the heat of passion and didn't care, one bit, if protection had been used—now full-blown pregnant, not knowing what to do.

Matt Miller's Trans Am eased up alongside the curb— few feet from where Melissa still lazily walked.

'Hey, cutie,' Matt said, window down. 'Need a lift?' The Trans Am was in a low-idle hum.

Melissa glanced up from the crack-filled sidewalk and ambled over. "We need to talk." She knew Matt could have a temper if things didn't work in his favor, on and off the field—and didn't know what his reaction would be concerning the baby that now grew strong inside.

'I'm late,' she said at the open window.

Matt flashed a seductive quarterback smile. 'Then hop in and I'll get you home.'

'I'm pregnant, Matt.'

'Well, is it mine?'

'Yes, Matt. You're my baby's father.'

'Are you sure?' Matt had scored more than just a touchdown.

'Yes, I'm sure,' Melissa cried.

'Calm down.' Matt opened the passenger side door. 'Get in. Let's talk.' Melissa obliged and got in. But soon wished she hadn't.

———

"Two weeks later, after Melissa was reported missing, I found her. Forsaken. In an alley. Behind a Dumpster. Stabbed. In cold blood. All because Matt Miller didn't want anyone finding out he had fooled around with a nine grader and got her pregnant. He was also scared that would've blown his OU scholarship." Paxton held Garrett in a heavy stare. "So, yeah, that kind of stuff you should expect. Day in, day out."

Soft soled shoes were back at the table. "More coffee?" Nancy placed the bill on the table, gentle smile. She had learned such pleasantries hooked in tips. A much needed adage when living off minimum wage.

"No thanks, Nancy." Paxton paid the bill, handsome tip, and walked with Garrett back outside.

After the glass door to the diner/coffee shop closed, Paxton added, "And if you're not careful, partner, faith in God can also wane."

The Crime Scene across the street still waited.

5

Paranoid fear always filled the rooms and halls of Hobbs Mental Health Center. It was a place where unfortunate souls, racked with mental illness, could no longer handle life's inner struggles, and who clawed away at spliced sanity, to be temporarily housed and cared for until some form of vague rational restraint, in mind and body, by way of heavy medication was regained, and the patient could finally return to society and waiting family members at home.

Hobbs Mental Health Center was also the place Heather Stockton signed in, Monday thru Friday, and did scheduled rounds as consoling counselor to those unfortunate souls racked with mental illness who could no longer handle life's inner struggles and clawed away at spliced sanity.

In no unsung terms, Heather Stockton represented a glimmer of hope to her patients. Her tender and caring demeanor drew even the most clinical case study, far away and safe for a while from cerebral torment and back to solid ground once more.

If not for Heather Stockton and her judicious talent in psychological matters—suicidal plans in impulse would have crept in, permanently stayed, and fatefully whispered, 'Go ahead. Do it.'" But aren't you glad you didn't, Kent?" Heather's smile cast a light a love upon the young man. Something he needed more than he truly knew.

Kent Wheaton had been a patient at Hobbs Mental Health Center for four days and had fought hard in the past fourteen years against the inner voices saying how he was scum and not the least bit worth saving. At least not by someone as caring as dear Heather Stockton. The voices also kept nudging Kent along in giving up hope, writing a final farewell note, and ending it, for sure this time, by sudden shotgun blast to the head, soon as he got out.

"Not really." There was a slight glint of worry in Kent's eyes because the wall he had so meticulously build around himself was slowly beginning to soften away. Which scared him.

"You don't really mean that." Heather began studying Kent's file. "Or else you wouldn't be here with me. Had you really wanted to end your life, you would have. Without question, you would have."

"Who's to say I won't next time."

Heather fished a legal pad and pen from the desk's top, front drawer and began the needed task of taking note. She took what Kent said as subtle warning before suicide.

"What kind of voices to you hear, Kent?" Quick, shorthand notes. "Male or female?"

"Does it matter. Male or female. Stupid question. Just stupid. Male or female. Wish they'd shut up though, tell you that. Hey, why'd you become a doctor, anyway?"

"You mean a counselor?"

"There's a difference?"

"Doctors write out scripts and operate," Heather joked. "Me, I just listen."

"What college did you got to?"

Sometimes if the subject at hand was briefly avoided, the patient would finally open up and begin to expel more than expected, and Heather knew this.

She paced herself, then pressed in.

"UCLA. Now back to you, Kent."

"Not much to get back to. Not like how it used to be."

"Let's talk about that. How it used to be."

"Let's not."

"I want you well. Not like how you are now."

"Where do you want to start?"

"When you first heard the voices."

"Voices?"

"The voices your folder here says you've been hearing."

"Since I was a kid. Around nine, I guess. Somewhere around there."

"And?"

"What more do you want to know?"

"Are the voices friendly or threatening?"

"You and your questions."

"Friendly or threatening, Kent?"

"Both."

"Both?" Heather made more quick, short hand notes— heavy scrawl across the page. She wanted everything down for future reference—later to be given to Dr. Sayer for full evaluation.

"Yeah, sometimes when the voices come, they're nice," Kent said. "Other times, straight-up mean."

"What do they sound like when the voices are mean?"

"Like men."

"And when the voices are nice?" More quick, short hand notes.

"Like women."

"When do the mean voices come, Kent?"

"Every day. Especially now, I'm older."

Heather tried to lighten the tension. "You're only twenty-three, Kent."

"Old enough to know, though."

"Know what?"

"Life won't get any easier. Not for me, that's for sure."

"You don't know."

"How do you know?"

Heather didn't. How could she? No one could predict which direction Kent's life would take. That would be like trying to properly gage an off-distant earthquake. And that off-distant earthquake, so to speak, before Heather, was Kent Wheaton—set ready, it seemed, to shake and tear apart at the seams.

"Is the mean voice speaking now, Kent?"

"I don't think so." Heavy concentration spread across his forehead—slight beads of perspiration sliding down throbbing temples. "Got a headache coming on. Got any aspirin?"

"Can't give you anything without Dr. Sayer's consent."

"The witch doctor?"

Kent's observation of the good doctor was far from flattering. Which was understandable. This had been Kent's eighth mental health facility over the years. He was at a desperate point in his life. What he needed was a heaven sent miracle—not prescribed drugs or group therapy sessions. All that had become as useful as sugar to a snake bite.

"I'm crazy, aren't I?"

"I don't like that word," Heather said, "but I do feel something happened to you when you were younger. Did something happen, Kent?"

There was a sudden flash in memory of being talked into a neighbor's house, up for sale, smashed in front window, by thirteen-year old Victor Thorton, twelve-year old Sammy Reniz, and sixteen-year old Gary Sager.

Kent felt strangled having that moment in time, when he was only nine, conjured back to life and replayed for analytical torture.

"I don't want to talk about it," he said, but slowly came around and began to tell Heather what had happened with those three other boys.

———

'I won't hurt you,' Victor said.

'This here is just a game. Right, gang?'

'Yep,' Sammy said, 'just a game.'

Gary was also in full agreement—twisted laugh.

'Now the game here,' Victor said, 'is called, Strip Down or Get Stuck.' His hand held a six-inch blade.

'So, strip down,' Gary said, 'or get stuck.' He was the worse of the three but lacked any IQ resonance to be much danger. Gary could hardly follow third grade directions, let alone mentally map out how to Kent alone there, in the house. Gary was a follower—not a leader. Not like how Victor was. Or, Sammy. When those two got together, it was full-on-no-holds-bar.

'Do it,' Sammy quipped, 'strip down or get stuck.' Kent was too out-numbered to take a stand and fight. Even if he could, his small frame was no match for the six-inch blade in Victor's hand.

Tears streaming down, Kent undressed—stripped down, lily-white naked. Embarrassment surged and struck hard.

'Hands off privates,' Victor ordered.

'No,' Kent whimpered, tears still streaming down.

'Really.' Victor lunged.

The six-inch blade plunged deep.

Kent grabbed his side—blood cascading through pale fingers.

'Ya really stabbed him, Vic,' Gary said.

Sammy laughed, 'The shrimp didn't do what was asked.'

Kent finally fell to his knees, losing more blood and in the most unbelievable pain. He had never been in a fight before—let alone stabbed. After all, he was only nine. And slowly dying.

A jingle-jangle of keys echoed from outside.

The front door opened.

'Best have a look inside,' realtor, Jane Winton told handy man, Jeff Morgan. 'Encase something else needs to be fixed, other than the front window.'

A low whisper came from Victor—'Let's bail, guys.' Stampede of heated steps.

Victor, Sammy, and Gary barged from the house, sliding door escape, hoped the concrete fence, and trailed off—down through a weed infested alley—leaving Kent still—'Bleeding,' Jane Winton said. 'He's bleeding bad. And just a child.'

'I'll get help.' Jeff Morgan raced to a neighboring house, told what had happened, and phoned the police; then an ambulance.

'Keep squeezing my hand,' Jane told Kent.

When help finally did arrive, Kent had lost enough blood, that he was fading in and out of sweet life; yet, still clung to Jane—tight hand-held squeeze.

'See,' she said, 'help's here.' Kent's eyes fluttered shut and the paramedics, now on the scene, eased him up and onto a gurney—out the house, and off to hospital—where it was two weeks, intense rehab because the six-inch blade had just barely missed Kent's spinal cord.

———

"You're lucky to even be walking," Heather said. She tried not to show emotion but it was hard not to. One's heart would have to be iced over and sealed in steel not to feel anything.

"I kinda know what it's like for a woman to be—"

"I understand," Heather interrupted. "So, after what happened is that when you started hearing voices?"

Kent said yes, that after that was when he first heard the voices rise up within and begin to speak.

"Those three ever get caught?"

"Yeah," Kent said, "they did."

"And?"

"Got sent upstate to a boys' home. Somewhere in Farmington. I think that's where they got sent. Somewhere in Farmington. I think."

"Fear they might find you again?"

"Yeah."

Heather's quick, shorthand notes stopped. She closed the notebook, pushed it aside and told Kent he did good, real good, and that they would talk again soon. Very soon.

Kent left the office.

Kid's been through a lot, Heather thought. *Sure has.*

Her thoughts then had her back to the night she wished had never happened.

———

'Hurry up, Heather. We're late.'

From the bathroom—'Okay.' After she had checked appearances, turned from the mirror, closed the door, and left the bathroom—Heather Stockton stood before, Xavier Torrez—her boyfriend of six months, met while doing a research paper in the library on Aldous Huxley and his futuristic novel, A Brave New World and how that sci-fi thriller could possibly, one day, become a feared reality—all of mankind eventually lumped into Omega, Beta, and Gama categories.

'Wow,' Xavier said. 'What a dress.'

Shyness blushed across rosy cheeks, unmarred and clear. Acne had never been an unwelcomed, infested fiend. In fact, puberty had been a rather easy road walked upon for Heather Stockton. Even her cycle wasn't something laced in mid-month dread.

'Ready?' Heather forced a smile.

Xavier didn't have to. 'Are you?'

'I don't know. Maybe not.'

'Not after I set this whole thing up, are you going to pull this now, Heather, understand?'

'Okay.'

That said, Heather Stockton collected herself, followed Xavier Torrez to his Buick Regal, got in—and was sped off into the night, to a sprawling mansion, deep in the Hollywood hills—where Heather walked onto her first and last seedy, adult film set.

———

Wish I had never done that. I knew better. But still, I did it.

Heather Stockton, naïve, fresh faced virgin and former high school honor grad from the Valley, had forgone better judgment that night and painfully lost her treasured innocence—forever captured in perverted detail, on film— pornographic trash that would later to be bought and purchased, behind-the-counter at all-night smut shops— far off the Interstate. Heather didn't know it but she was a fave among dirty minded truck drivers, nationwide.

Why didn't I just tell Xavier no? Wasn't like he was my soul mate. True. Xavier had been someone only to pass time with and not to get too wrapped up in. Or so Heather thought.

After that regretful night in the Hollywood hills, Xavier Torrez wasn't such an easy rid.

He hounded Heather to the point of dark obsession. Wherever she was, whatever time of day, Xavier eventually slithered there, too. That was exactly how Heather came to see Xavier Torrez—a cold-blooded, reptilian creature— void of love and caring warmth. All that coursed through his mind: how to inflict emotional pain upon naïve, fresh faced virgins and former high school honor grads from the Valley. Like, Heather Stockton.

Xavier Torrez didn't get another chance with another girl, like Heather. Not after the restraining order was filed.

Strangely enough, after that, Xavier Torrez pulled a vanishing act and disappeared.

For good, Heather thought. She longed for home—where a nice, hot bath would be drawn to relax away the high-stress day.

Heather Stockton was beat; not only from the in-depth counsel given to Kent Wheaton, but from also remembering her own youth-induced trauma.

Maybe I should call someone?

That someone who Heather thought of phoning was none other than Mitch Taylor, once Cody Holt's youth pastor from Los Angeles (this, Heather didn't know) and the one who wrote the front page inscription in his New American Standard bible—and the one who was now the newly appointed pastor at Northside Baptist Church in Hobbs, New Mexico.

Yes, Hobbs, New Mexico.

6

Exhaustion and fatigue finally merged and climaxed.
Cody Holt had been on the road for sixteen hours.
No note. No cell phone. No bodyguard protection. And
no call to agent Derek Harris, to notify in case of off-
set emergency.

No one knew where Cody Holt was or where he was
headed. For the first time, in a long time, he was on his
own—far from Hollywood and its false façade of harmonious life.

I need sleep.

Hazel eyes watered with tears and the road ahead
became a dizzy blur. White lines crisscrossed and weaved,
like a heated mirage, atop scorching desert sand.

On the left, in the distance, was The Red Roof Inn.

Cody took the next exit, cruised the BMW up to the
lobby, shut the engine off, got out, and ambled slowly up to
the entrance.

He went in.

No one was at the front desk. Of course, such late hour as it was, might have been reason why.

3:00 am, showed the clock on the far-left wall.

"Didn't know it was so late," Cody whispered, then noticed a small, silver bell. He lightly tapped it.

The door behind the front desk squeaked open.

A haggard looking old man, coarse white whiskers peppered across his thinly gaunt face, wobbled forth—leaned his cane against the desk, and rubbed yellow sleep from his dull, gray eyes. They seemed as if any and all color had been mysteriously drained clean and replaced with an odd pewter hue.

"What can I do ya for?"

"Just a single," Cody yawned.

The old man cast a quick glance out the window. "Dat der y'r car?"

Who's else would it be? Cody thought, then said, "Yeah, she's mine."

"Must be nice." The old man snagged a registration form and asked Cody for his driver's license, and how many days/nights to be spent at The Red Roof Inn.

"Just tonight."

Deep chuckle. "Ya mean, this morning."

"Whatever." Cody reached for his wallet. But stopped.

"Problem?" the old man asked.

There was. If Cody showed his driver's license, his identity would be blown, and no longer a sly, hidden secret.

"We makin' a transaction here, or what?"

"Sorry. Been on the road a while." Cody finally slid his driver's license across the counter.

Eyes not blinking, the old man looked long and hard at Cody's driver's license. "No, not "the" Chaz Spivey, are ya?"

"Yeah, I am."

"Heck, no charge, then."

"You don't have to," Cody said.

"It ain't no problem," the old man said. "Heck, ya probably use ta da kinda treatment, anyhow. Tell me, though, what's it's like ta be famous, like how ya are?"

"More problems than can be explained." Cody glanced to his left and noticed something, like a large fish tank, covered with a blanket. "What's that?"

The old man turned and walked around the front desk. "Wanna see?"

"Why not."

When the blanket was pulled off, the old man slowly backed up. So did, Cody.

Two medium-size Western diamond back rattlesnakes shook rattle tipped tails and slithered around one other. The larger viper crawled to a corner and wrapped itself up in a threatening, S shape—ready to strike. The other, rather smaller viper, stayed put—but just as deadly.

"I usually charge twenty big ones, ta lift dat der blanket. But not for you, Mr. Spivey. Nope, not for you, Mr. Spivey."

"Well, thanks," Cody said, got the plastic room key from the old man, went back out to the BMW, snagged luggage that lay next to a container of Peak anti-freeze, and shut the trunk.

That's when an icy voice came from behind.

Think you can run from this? From what you said that night, before the mirror. Remember?

Cody turned. "Who's there?"

The icy voice said again—*Think you can run from this? From what you said that night, before the mirror. Remember?*

A rancid smell of sulfur permeated the thick Arizona air and Cody gagged—mind a marred mess—all cloudy and not understanding, at first—until the memory of that night surfaced again—at the mirror—cursing God. Then all became clear.

"I'm going to hell," Cody whispered, terror-filled voice.

Yes, you are. No hope left. Not for you, Cody Holt. Or I should say, Chaz Spivey. You're done in. Sure are. Think this bad, just wait until you breathe your last. Then you'll truly know what bad is. All this is just a warm up. Act one. But don't worry. Many more to go, that's for sure.

Aside from that icy voice, fiery laughter soon echoed deep in Cody's ear and threw him to his knees. Which didn't go unnoticed.

The old man limped outside.

"Ya okay, Mr. Spivey? Here…Let's me get ya ta yr room."

The old man lifted Cody up, arm around waist, and guided him to Room 36. Which was Cody Holt's real age—not the six year difference, Tracy Powers, Cody's

Hollywood publicist, had printed in the birthday section of national newspapers, each year.

The plastic key was swiped down, and the door to Room 36 slowly opened.

The smell of staleness waived by.

Cody coughed. The smell was too much—too soon.

"Sorry, maid service here's been kinda weak." The old man laid Cody down on the single bed. "What happened out der?"

Cody just shrugged. How could he say he heard a voice that dropped him to his knees, without coming off as if having no toys in the attic?

The old man added, "Phone's right der, on da nightstand, by da bed, here. Just ring zero if ya need anything, Mr. Spivey." The old man was now at the nightstand, arthritic hand opening the top drawer. "An' here's a bible if ya want sumpin' ta read."

Like that will do you any good.

Fiery laughter echoed.

Cody raised his head. "Do you hear that?"

"Hear what?"

"Never mind." Cody silently cried for some form of nirvana to come and shut out the ever-present and taunting laugh-stricken voice. But no form of nirvana came—just the need for deep sleep.

"Well," the old man said, "I'll leave ya be."

The door closed, and Cody heard that icy voice sing a line from a famous Gordon Lightfoot song—*Sundown, you better take care, If I find you'd been creepin' 'round my back stair.*

Deep sleep soon had Cody its grip and coaxed him far under.

It was a dreamless slumber.

7

"**G**one?"
        "Yeah, gone."
"Well, were do you think he is?"
"I don't know."
"You're his agent, Derek."
"And you're his publicist, Tracy."
"Have you told anyone else this?"
"No."
"Good. Don't. Just hang tight."
"Hang tight?"
"Yes."
"Something's not right. I can feel it, Tracy."
"You're over re-acting, Derek."
"America's top heartthrob is nowhere to be had."
"Doesn't mean something bad's happened."
"What else could it mean?"

"Chaz is probably housed up and being mothered by some slender-waist beauty."

"I don't think so, Tracy."

All this hash-tag talk had worn Derek down. He didn't even want to discuss it anymore, but had to. His numero uno client, Chaz Spivey, was nowhere to be had. Then there was still negotiation, concerning *Wine and Roses* to be ironed out. If it could. No actor in sight, no—Lights/ Camera/Action. *Wine and Roses* would be nixed before even taking flight on set.

Tracy walked from behind her desk and sat down. "Like I said, Chaz is probably housed up and being mothered by some slender-waist beauty."

"There seemed something so icy in his house."

"You were in his house?"

Jealously surged.

Sure, Tracy Powers had signed the dotted line as publicist to be in working relations with Chaz Spivey, but that didn't halt heated desire from rising up for her top A-list Hollywood client. Tracy wished nothing more than to be the one housing up Chaz Spivey and mothering him. That little outing, if it ever came to pass, would cross an unseen line.

Toss work and "hush-hush" bedtime cravings together and things are never the same. Tracy and Chaz's working relationship was harmonious enough without intimate passion thrown in the mix. But how Tracy wished.

"Why did he do that?" She was back behind her desk. "Give you a key to his house."

"In case something like this happened, I guess." The notion then hit Derek. "You love, Chaz, don't you, Tracy?"

She laughed, "He's somewhat handsome, but we have a working relationship. That's all, Derek. Anyway, nothing happened to, Chaz. Stop worrying."

"Maybe we should hire a P.I. Just to be safe."

"Know what would happen if we did that?"

"Media hysteria. You're right, Tracy. Just hang tight, like you said."

"Look, if Chaz doesn't show in the next few days, then yeah, hire a P.I. But Derek, it won't come to that. Trust me, okay."

He was at the door. "Just hang tight, right?"

Tracy smiled. "Just hang tight, Derek."

He nodded, said thanks for listening, and left the office. He was running late for his first appointment with Dr. O'Connor. He was the leading Los Angeles psychologist and mental advisor to all who could fit the bill—mostly those with deep and wide pockets.

The appointment had been called and scheduled in by Amber because Derek just couldn't find the guts to do so. All he saw was heavy doses of heavy drugs and jolting, electroshock therapy that, he feared, would leave him brain dead and numb inside, faltering far beyond the cuckoo's nest—that deeply wounded place where the outside world no longer moves in fluid motion.

Suddenly, Derek popped his head back in. "Are you sure, Tracy?"

"Would you trust me," she said. "Just hang tight, like I said."

"All right."

The door closed again. Derek was gone, again.

You can hang tight, Tracy thought. *But I'm hiring my own P.I. I'll be the one to save Chaz. Not you, Derek.*

Seven digits were dialed.

Call roamed.

Then—"Yeah." The voice was rough and masculine. Three packs of smokes, each day, twenty years strong, had tarnished Jim Jackson's voice to a heavy, nicotine rasp.

"I need something." Tracy twirled a lock of her auburn hair, streaked warm in deep butterscotch highlights. Even on the phone, Tracy fell into female temptress.

"What kind of something?"

Tracy explained how Chaz Spivey was nowhere to be had, and if word got out, the media frenzy that would soon ensue.

"So, keep your mouth shut about what I just told you, Jim."

"That might be fun, seeing this town go crazy over some pansy-pampered actor, like Chaz Spivey." Jim Jackson had a heavy disdain for all things Hollywood. But that which he disdained most, paid the bills in full. Jim Jackson had been going at it like this, as Private Investigator, since the early Eighties, decade of life lived in excessive excess and gluttonous greed.

"Just tell me if you're in or out, Jim?"

He knew the money would be ripe. "Sure. Why not. I'm in."

Tracy said she would call later with full details on where, when, and what should go down in trying to track Chaz Spivey's location.

"In the meantime, Jim, sit tight."

"Will do." He clasped his cell phone shut. The call was dropped.

Tracy smiled. Her thoughts raced—*When Chaz finds out it was me who first went looking for him, he won't have any choice, but love me.*

Her thoughts soon drifted to when she had first met, Cody Holt.

⸻

'You need a publicist, honey.'

Cody turned. 'Really?'

'Sure do,' Tracy smiled.

Derek Harris introduced, 'Cody Holt, this is, Tracy Powers. Best publicist in the Biz. Tracy Powers, this is, Cody Holt. Furture Hollywood heartthrob.'

Tracy fell into temptress mode. 'Honey, you need a name change. Cody Holt really won't do. Will it, Derek?'

'We're working on that, right, Cody?'

'Haven't come up with anything catchy, yet. But like Derek said, we're working on it.'

'Well, I'll leave you two to talk shop.'

Derek blended in with the rest of the bigwigs at the Industry party and left Cody and Tracy alone, to see if they were a good fit.

A high-ranking agent like Derek Harris was important; but so was an astute publicist, like Tracy Powers. She knew how to navigate the treacherous waters of movie-star-image-making. Without an astute publicist, like Tracy Powers, an actor like, Cody Holt, would be adrift and lost in a dark sea of Hollywood, public relations. Something Tracy Powers knew well. And something, Cody Holt, by night's end, would soon realize.

'So, what name would you tag me with?'

Tracy sized up her future prospect. 'Well, you don't look like a, Cody Holt, that's for sure.'

'What do I look like, then?' Cody got into, "playing the game." Something to be endured, if any form of success was to ever be had.

'Let me see.'

'Well?'

'Give me a second,' Tracy grinned. 'Coming up with a saleable name, isn't easy.'

'I'm waiting,' Cody winked.

Tracy flashed a gorgeous smile. The name had finally rung inside her head. 'Chaz Spivey.'

Cody laughed. 'Really?'

'Casting directors hear that name, then see the guy behind that name…Well…Well, is all I can say…Chaz Spivey.'

'Chaz Spivey? Are sure?'

'Keep saying it.'

Cody did. Soon, he saw it like Tracy did. 'You're right.'

'I know.'

Cody scanned the room and waved Derek back over.

'Got the name we were searching for.'

'What name?' Derek asked.

'Chaz Spivey,' Tracy chimed in. 'Isn't it beautiful?'

Derek wasn't so sure about the name. A great name, like great look, is key in soaring far beyond other actors, dead-set on the same chosen path to fame. If name doesn't fit look, like the one Cody Holt possessed—then forget it. More promising Hollywood careers have choked, died off, and vanished, for nothing less than wrong name tagged at the bottom of an 8X10 glossy, white-board-framed headshot.

Finally, Derek agreed, 'Chaz Spivey does have a certain ring.'

'Settled, then?' Tracy smiled.

'Far as I'm concerned, it is,' Cody said.

'Chaz Spivey it is, then.' Derek shook Cody's hand, and Cody turned to, Tracy.

'Think you could find room for another client, like me?'

Tracy smiled. 'Would be a pleasure to be your new publicist, Mr. Spivey.'

That night signaled the transformation of Cody Holt into Chaz Spivey. And Tracy Powers flowering love for both: Cody Holt as wounded-like orphan; and Chaz Spivey— soon to be Hollywood's newest insert into colossal, worldwide fame.

Tracy now wondered if a huge injustice had been done?

After Cody Holt accepted his new name and growing fame—changes surfaced. Not so much with Cody, although there were minor ones, here and there. It was the people around him and how they treated him, that changed. They always went a little too far to please and accommodate, whatever may have been mentioned in passing.

One time, after a brief mention to newly hired assistant, Rebecca Newton, of really wanting season tickets with court side seats to the Lakers—those prized, season tickets popped up at Derek's office.

That, and whatever music act Cody was into at the time, was no problem booking a private meet-and-greet and one-on-one jam session. Along the way, Cody had learned, back in high school, rudiment guitar chords; and later, slapping bass lines. He even went as far to form his own "little" band of misfits—Nite-Nite. Sadly, they were a much less talented version of Duran Duran; but still sported the make-up, coifed hair, New Romantic style—leather trousers, boots, headbands, and sashes, too.

That short-lived venture into noisy entertainment eventually lead Cody Holt to Mr. NcNaire's drama class.

Which eventually lead to Derek Harris.

Which eventually lead to Tracy Powers.

Which eventually lead Cody Holt to Chaz Spivey.

To eventually become Chaz Spivey.

To eventually be, nowhere to be had.

Nowhere no one knew of, as of yet.

I should just call off the search, Tracy thought. *Probably more harm than good will come of it. And I've probably done enough harm to, Chaz…I mean, Cody.*

Still, with all she knew, Tracy couldn't bring herself to pick up the phone and do what was so desperately needed.

The phone stayed put, untouched.

Tracy shut the lights off and left the office.

8

The recess bell at Wilson Elementary rang and quickened each student's attention in Jessica Harris's first grade class down to a rumbling anticipation for the playground—that special place where imaginations take flight. Also, that special thirty-minute break before lunch when precious, little Jessica got to spend time with friends her own age and talk, after an intense game of hide-and-seek, about what they would do when they were all grown up and on their own and had to contend with the same things all grown-ups do.

But not today. Such grown-up talk as that wasn't what was on Jessica's mind.

What pounded away at her, since it happened—was the man in her room, who claimed, he said, to be an angel—a heaven sent angel.

Jessica was winded and panting from running to her secret hiding place when she spotted Geoffrey Sullivan. After she caught her breath, she walked up.

"You believe in Angels, Geoffrey?"

"Guess so," he said. "The bible says they're there, so I guess they are." He turned to run. "Tag, you're it."

"Wait," Jessica said, "hold on. I've seen one."

Geoffrey stopped. "Seen what?"

"An angel."

"Joke's up, Jess."

"Geoffrey Sullivan, this isn't a joke."

"Sure sounds like a joke to me."

"I saw an angel in my room, the other night."

"What'd this angel look like then, huh?"

"Heavenly."

"You're gonna have to do better than that because whenever I see ice cream, I think that's heavenly. So, how I see your angel, Jess, is like one big ol' scoop of Ben and Jerry's, Chunky Monkey."

"Who I saw in my room wasn't a big ol' scoop of Ben and Jerry's, and he wasn't no chunky monkey, either. He was an angel."

"So you say, Jess."

"I don't want to be friends anymore with you."

Jessica ran off the playground and back inside Wilson Elementary to the "little girls" room, last unit, and latched the stall shut.

Tears rolled down in heavy streaks. Jessica wiped her cheeks.

She then heard—"Don't cry."

Jessica immediately recognized the voice and quickly unlatched the stall, flung open the door, and came out.

There, standing tall was the angel from the night before.

The angelic being lifted his hand and swiped it through the air.

"Why'd you do that?" Jessica was in awe.

"To briefly stop time," the angel said, "so we can talk."

"Am I in trouble?"

The angel smiled. "No, you're not in trouble, Jessica."

"Good, because for a minute, I thought God had my number."

"No, but God, the Father does know who you are, Jessica."

"Really?"

The angel smiled again. "The Father knew you before the foundation of the earth, Jessica. Just as I did."

"You?"

"Yes."

"I don't understand."

"One day, you will."

"But not today, huh?"

"No, Jessica, not today."

"Are you my guardian angel?"

"Yes, I am, Jessica."

The angel with Jessica wasn't the only spiritual being who could briefly stop time. Nothing could be done. Jessica was frozen in a time-stand-still.

"You're about to break the rules," an ungodly fallen angel said. "You're not suppose to, in any way, physically influence, anyone. Ever. Even her, you're special, "little" pet project."

"Jessica is not a pet project."

"Save it for someone who really cares, Miguel."

"Why are you here, Azur?"

He was a fallen angel who had thrown in his lot with Satan in the first earth age. Now, just one of many, Lucifer's minions who whisper and dangle luring temptation upon earth's fallen spiritual state, to keep the human race—man, woman, and child—in constant, bitter fright over any and all silent plight, cried out in prayer.

"Same as you, Miguel, to influence. But I'm playing by the rules. Unlike, you."

"I haven't crossed any line."

"I can show you how."

"Leave," Miguel commanded. "Now, Azur."

"I'll just be back, you know that. Hey, let's find a heard of swine, possess them, and drown them in a river. Whatcha say, huh?"

"Leave!"

Like that, Azur was gone.

Before Miguel brought time back to its original state, he left Jessica, walked onto the playground, found Geoffrey Sullivan, and whispered, "What Jessica told you about me is true."

Miguel raised his hand, palm down, and swiped it through the air again, as if slicing through fog.

Time resumed.

The recess bell rang.

The playground scattered clear.

Children then ran in line and waited to be ushered back to class—where mathematics, science, English, and world history fundamentals rested within crisp, clean bound pages of newly issued textbooks that would be cracked back open again and delved into for up-coming tests, next week. The teachers at Wilson Elementary prided themselves in proper education that would propel each student in Mrs. Graham's class, far past ready for second grade.

No one saw, including Mrs. Graham, Jessica poke her head out of the "little girls" room and rush, last in line, behind Geoffrey Sullivan.

He turned and said, "You know, Jess, I thought about it, and I believe you. Don't really know how, but you *did* see an angel in your room, the other night."

"Thank you."

"Still friends?"

Jessica flashed her missing-front-tooth smile. "Still friends."

The two first graders, pinkies clasped tight together, hands swinging back and forth, walked back into class.

Mrs. Graham, as always, waited behind her podium. The textbook, History: A World's Study was open and ready to be delved into again.

9

On-set madness isn't so on-set. Not at first.

A slow progression that begins without any first-sign symptoms to gage the war to come is how it starts.

Like most who suffer this silent but lethal mental intrusion upon self, the first-sign symptoms don't really seem at all like first-sign symptoms—more like nagging hassles to darken days and worry-fill starry nights about becoming overly concerned about checking and re-checking door locks; phone connections; TV signal; room temperature; extension cords; drier sheets; window panes; CD player; bills (paid or un-paid); razors; shaving cream; toilet paper— along with toothpaste and toothbrush. Or, nothing of the likes, at all.

What sets one off into the vast unknown wilds of the mind, so as to get wrapped tight within cerebral cobwebs, really defies any forthright description in sane logic. Each person is different. Thus, each person suffers different. But suffer, each person does—along with friends and family. On that insane, disturbed ride—they to, do go.

Just as Derek and Amber were painfully about to find out.

"It'll be okay," she told him. "Probably like how you said, work, and how it got to you, and all. Nothing more than that."

Derek breathed. "I hope so."

Oddly enough, Don Mclean's song, *Vincent* painted the air in sweet melody from octagon shaped ceiling speakers. Mclean's voice eerily filled the waiting room that lead to the door which, once passed, lead down the hall to Dr. O'Connor's spacious office.

Derek eyed the clock. Time was 8:50. Ten minutes until the dreaded inevitable. "It's almost nine," he told Amber. "Let's sneak out."

"We're going to take care of what ills you, Derek. We're not sneaking out."

"I'm glad I married you for your body and not your way with words."

Amber gave a weak smile. Where she was with Derek, and where Derek was mentally had placed secret strain upon Amber, and seemed to be affecting the very body Derek jokingly said he had married her for.

Early in the morning, two hours before Derek woke, Amber had hugged the toilet in dry heave pain. Nothing came up—other than salty bile, which caused another sudden blitz of dry heave pain—which caused more salty bile to rise.

Dr. O'Connor was suddenly on the scene in the reception area. He was without secretarial help and preferred to work alone. He and private solace, over the years, had become dear, close friends.

He motioned for Derek and Amber to follow. They did. The door to the office closed.

O'Connor offered chairs. "Go ahead and sit, so we can start."

"Which scares me." Derek finally sat. So did Amber. She squeezed his hand as if to say, 'I'm here for you.' "Don't be nervous." O'Connor knew that wouldn't come be. In his twenty-plus years in trying to crack the mental health dilemma, O'Connor had never once seen a first-time patient at ease in exercising personal demons in open therapy; and Derek Harris, it seemed, would be no different. O'Connor had sadly come to one finite conclusion: the mental health dilemma would remain stagnate in never being explained away as nothing more than harsh chemical imbalances within the brain.

The medical community has, as of yet, no fundamental proof nor sound doctrine to whitewash, why one suddenly, without recourse, plummets passed the preverbal wormhole of lunacy and winds up behind four padded, highly institutionalized walls, monitored by security cameras. O'Connor tried his best to explain this; yet, the explanation came off more like jumble-jimble-mash than anything else.

"In English," Derek laughed; then thought, *I need more cowbell!*

"If you do, indeed, suffer from a mental illness," O'Connor explained, "there will be no magic bullet for you."

"Been reading the Warren Commission?" Amber smiled.

O'Connor returned the smile and began the rigors of in-depth, personal questioning. Exact thing, Derek feared. Regardless, the questioning began.

"Explain what's going on."

"Lately, things seem to be closing in around me."

O'Connor asked for a better explanation and was set to take careful note, pen carefully pressed down upon the lined paper of a legal pad. He glanced back up at Derek and waited for his reply.

Derek couldn't put into words what caused his mental wheels to burn white-hot, off kilter. Which brought fear. Derek Harris was in the business of clear-cut, Hollywood negotiation. Not lose-lip, vague talk—like how it was going with O'Connor.

"Take your time," Amber urged.

"Yes," O'Connor agreed, "take your time, Derek."

He just sat there.

Amber coaxed, "You're going to have open up."

O'Connor waited, pen still carefully pressed down upon the lined paper of the legal pad.

"I'm afraid I'll lose my job, as an agent." Derek finally said.

""That's right," O'Connor said, "you work in Hollywood."

"As an agent, don't forget," Amber added. Even a wife married to a power player, like Derek Harris, sometimes makes known, how her husband should be seen in higher standing than most, and treated as such. In Hollywood, be it actor, agent, writer, or trophy wife to all three—covetous weight gets thrown around; and if opportunity presents itself—emotions are sometimes cut deep and to the quick— all under the brutal, cut-throat guise of, as the saying goes: business as usual.

Amber roped back her ego. "I'm sorry. This is my husband's time. Not mine." She squeezed Derek's hand again.

O'Connor could tell something was about to tear apart if an intervention of the heart wasn't done. This wouldn't be the first time, out the gate, he switched from shrink to marriage counselor.

"I think this session would not only greatly benefit, Derek, but you too, Mrs. Harris. Would that be fine with you?"

Amber expressed how much she wanted that. So did, Derek. They were both finally in agreement on something. The session progressed nicely from there, without conflict, centered mostly on Derek and that chilled feeling of how things were closing in, all around, and the fear of losing his job.

O'Connor explained further that panic attacks intertwined within anxiety was, more than likely, Derek's problem, and medication could be prescribed to help even out that creepy-crawl feeling Derek said was suddenly there—one day, without warning—had simply just shown up—like an infectious virus in blood.

"Which is how these things happen to everyone," O'Connor said. "Now," he added, "about meds. I think—"

"Not," Derek interrupted.

Amber leaned in. "Don't jump off so soon. If Dr. O'Connor suggests meds then follow his prescribed order. More than just your job depends on this, Derek."

"Your wife's right."

Derek nodded and kissed Amber's hand. Her seven carat, pink champagne diamond ring cast a rainbow prism of light above Derek's left eye.

Sudden thoughts of Jessica and the mishap she remembered not, of falling from her crib to the floor below and being rushed to the hospital for seven carefully placed stitches above her own left eye, five and a half year ago— hit Derek. Amber was sure-fire right, how more than just Derek's job depended on the med situation. Precious, little Jessica also had to be brought off the fence, so to speak, and lovingly added to the equation. Derek breathed. "What kind of meds?"

"Zoxin," O'Connor said, "new to the market, and just out."

Amber intersected, "Side effects?"

"Yeah," Derek said. "What about those?"

"Mild," O'Connor informed.

Derek squirmed. It seemed O'Connor held back vital information concerning this new drug to the market. Then again, wasn't like he said: 'don't worry about side effects because there won't be any.' No, O'Connor didn't say that; but didn't add anything, either, to rest and settle chary fears. Like the ones Derek strongly felt coming on.

Sweat trickled down his brow.

"Am I crazy?"

Amber voiced, "Derek!"

"You're not crazy," O'Connor assured.

"Good," Derek said, "then I might reconsider all this med business, not to take any."

"No, you won't reconsider," Amber said.

The session had now shifted to high-conflict. Derek was no longer sure about any of this, anymore. Not like how he was, mere seconds ago. He wanted out and told O'Connor so.

"Out of your life?" O'Connor's hand was by the phone, ready to dial out. If Derek did, as he eluded to, wanted out of his life, O'Connor had no choice but to take that as a prelude cry before suicide, and dispatch an emergency 5150 call to the LAPD.

"Not out of my life," Derek said, handkerchief to brow, "just this office."

Tears hung heavy in Amber's eyes. "Then do what O'Connor wants with the meds."

"Okay," Derek finally agreed. "But I want to know all side effects to this Zoxin drug. There has to be more than just mild, like you said."

"Not really," O'Connor said. "The side effects are mild."

Amber asked, "But mild how?"

"Maybe more sleep than usual. And Derek's appetite may also increase." O'Connor wrote out the script. "Other than that, he should have no problems."

"If he does?"

"Call me," O'Connor told Amber. "But I really feel nothing other than what I mentioned, will happen."

The script was handed over.

Derek took it.

"Twice a day?" he asked, and stowed the handkerchief back in his pocket.

"Yes," O'Connor said. "One pill, twice daily."

"For how long?" Amber asked.

O'Connor leaned forward. "You probably don't want to hear—"

""How long?" Derek asked.

O'Connor leaned back. "The rest of your life. Understand, what you're up against, isn't a simple headache where an aspirin will suffice. If your anxiety isn't dealt with now, Derek, your condition may get worse."

"Worse than I am now?"

O'Connor said, "Possibly, yes."

"He's not that bad off." Amber slipped her hand around Derek's arm. "Maybe a little on edge, but that's it. Nothing that would constitute meds for the rest of his life."

O'Connor cleared his throat. "It's hard for family members to accept the fact, something like what Derek is going through, can't be completely eradicated or cleansed away. The mind gets sick, like the rest of the body. Think of it Amber, like Derek having high blood pressure."

"But I don't have high blood pressure." Derek lashed out, "I'm crazy!"

Amber now knew, just what Derek faced. What she didn't know was how Derek would eventually handle, what seemed, to have completely over taken. Something had to intervene, other than O'Connor just sitting there.

All he knew to tell Derek was, one pill, twice daily—no more, no less.

"Back to that?" Derek said.

"For now," O'Connor said. "Then we'll see."

"See what?" Amber asked.

"How Derek is in a month."

That didn't sit well. But what else could was he to do? There was no other avenue to turn down.

"Okay," he said. "One pill, twice daily. No more, no less." Amber kissed his flushed cheek.

O'Connor glanced at his Rolex. "Time's up." He began penciling in Derek's next appointment. "Tenth of December good with you?"

"Fine," Derek agreed.

"Good," O'Connor said. "See you then." He was out of his seat. "Here," he added, "let me walk you both, back out."

Derek and Amber followed, left the office, got in the Lexus and drove off—headed for the 101.

They were both thankful Jessica was still in school and wouldn't arrive back home for another three hours.

Derek and Amber both needed some much desired time alone.

But that brief moment of pleasure would not sustain nor stop what would soon unfold.

The Harris household was about to be rocked.

10

Worry grinded away at Curtis Paxton. Talent to know exactly what Amanda's heart desired by way of gift still had him miffed. Even after fifteen-years of blissful marriage, that did nothing to ease Curtis's anxious toil, if whatever token of affection bought would bring forth the same warmth to Amanda's face as when that first date commenced into a lengthy courtship, then later—marriage. A happy marriage. No true emotional damaged fight that wasn't able to be worked through and come out stronger than before.

Every time Curtis and Amanda fought, after a brief spell of cooling off, the sudden pull to embrace and make up, always brought them together again—as if the fight had been nothing more than a distant, passing breeze.

Really hope she likes these. Curtis opened a small, black velvet jewelry box—his deep gaze transfixed and unwavering upon the newly purchased diamond earrings from Zales which shimmered bright in vague twinkles from the 100 watt bulb that still burned bright.

Curtis had explained to Amanda, after the honeymoon, how danger lurked in wait for a woman alone at home at night without some bright beacon to ward off possible intruders—even if that woman's husband was a cop starting out, and seven years later, made Detective yet was still late, most night's coming home. Like tonight.

Curtis shut the small, black velvet jewelry box, stuffed it in his pocket, opened the front door, and walked in. Two more years in payment, and the Paxton's would finally have legal ownership to their modest abode.

The front door shut and took Amanda by surprise.

She turned from the oven and ran up and kissed Curtis.

This always made him grin.

On the streets, Paxton was Curtis's formal Detective moniker. None was more professional and "by the book," than he. But at home—with concerns of a "black cloud" world still seething with crime—Curtis cherished every breath spent in the arms of his beloved wife, Amanda.

Here lately, though—faith in God was almost ice cold for Curtis because the criminal sins on LA streets weighed heavy—like vast bulks of sturdy-strong solidity that drains off all energy.

He pushed that aside. Something more pending now needed attention than what possibly lay in wait, in shadows on the LA streets.

The time had come.

The small, black velvet jewelry box was laid in Amanda's hand.

"Open it," Curtis teased.

Amanda's eyes went wild at the sight of the diamond earrings. "It's not even our anniversary, yet."

"Couldn't wait to give them to you. Hope you—"

"I love them." Amanda came close. "But not as much as I love you." Her passion consumed Paxton with a tender kiss.

He returned the passion with a tender kiss of his own. Eyes shut tight, they were lost again within the feeling they had for one another while dating.

The timer buzzed.

"Dinner's done." Amanda turned from Curtis, slipped on a pot holder, and got the lasagna out the oven. "Let's eat."

They made their way to the dining room.

The table was already set—plates in place.

Curtis smiled. He loved how Amanda always cared for his needs—be it food or physical. Amanda had become Curtis's world, and it had been that way since he first saw her—sixteen-years ago—at Toni & Guy.

———

'Care who cuts your hair?' The receptionist didn't looked up from the appointment book. Her sleek, graduated bob drew heavy attention from Curtis.

'Who cuts yours?'

'Amanda.'

'Is she here.'

The receptionist looked up from the appointment book. 'I can pencil you in. Is that fine?' Curtis said that would be great and took a seat to wait. It wasn't long before Amanda appeared from the break room and told him she would be his stylist for the day; then signaled for an assistant.

'This is Andre.' Amanda took a step back. 'He will shampoo your hair today.' Curtis was led by Andre to a shampoo bowel—sat down, relaxed, while Andre turned on the water, wet Curtis's hair and lathered it up.

A perfumed fragrance engulfed the room.

'What kind of shampoo is that?'

'Gentle Cleansing. It's a best seller, here.' Andre turned the faucet on.

The lather was rinsed clean; then a strong scent of peppermint rose.

'What's that?'

Andre gave a half-cocked grin. 'Toni & Guy's special Peppermint Treatment. I think you'll like it.' A heft amount of white conditioner slathered Curtis's hair.

Then—'Wow,' Curtis voiced. A strong tingle stimulated his scalp. 'Stuff's strong. Like Wasabi for the hair.' Andre grinned, rinsed off the conditioner, covered Curtis's hair with a towel, and lead him back over to Amanda.

She was at her station, tinkering with a pair of razor sharp, Joewell shears.

'What were you thinking, how you'd like your hair?'

'Have at it. I trust you.' Actually it Curtis's heart that was beginning to trust Amanda.

She smiled and began.

Toni & Guy, being an upper echelon salon, rarely, if ever, does a client say, 'have at it.' Patrons that frequent the salon are anything but nonchalant when it comes to their hair and how it's cut.

Toni & Guy has a reputation that surpasses name and logo. Not everyone who inquires gets hire. Toni & Guy are guarded and slightly jaded to hire just any stylist.

A rigorous weeding out process of potential talent takes place. If a stylist is then hired, they are relegated down to lowly assistant anywhere from six months to nine months; and in that six to nine month gestation period as assistant, each Tuesday night at Toni & Guy headquarters, selected models' hair are cut into whatever stylish coif that week's demands require.

Amanda had no problem with any required demands and tested out, three weeks ahead of schedule. Her talent, not just to cut hair, but shape hair—rivaled even the most masterful stylist at Toni & Guy.

She was done and handed Curtis a mirror, unlocked the barber chair, and swiveled him around.

'I love it.' Curtis smiled.

"No you didn't," Amanda teased.

"Did, to," Curtis said, mouth full of lasagna. "I always love how you cut my hair."

His gaze left Amanda.

"What's wrong?" she asked Silence.

"Don't do this. Don't shut me out." Her stare kept solid vigil over, Curtis. "Something's got you worried."

He finally said—"God."

"God?"

"Yes," Curtis said, "God."

"Why does God have you worried?"

"Because I wonder if He's really up there."

"Where else would God be?"

"I don't know. Do you?"

"Yes, I do." Amanda began clearing off the table.

"How you know for sure?"

"I just do." Amanda cradled the plates to the sink and turned on the water.

Oddly enough, the china seemed baptized clean.

When she was done, she put the china back in the cabinet and turned to Curtis.

He sat silent-still, there in the dining room.

Amanda went to him.

"You okay?" She rested in his lap.

"I don't think so."

"Why?"

Curtis took a deep breath. "I think I may have lost whatever faith I have in, God." Tears rose.

"What brought this on?"

"I don't really know." Curtis's eyes still glistened with tears. "I just don't feel God, anymore. If I ever really did.

I mean, when I was kid, yeah, sure. But now…Now, I just don't know, anymore. Do you feel, God?"

What could someone say to that? That the presence of the Holy Father is felt continually, without restraint? Are mere mortal humans even allowed such Divine access to heavenly realms, let alone the Holy Father, other than by prayer? These question were what ate at, Curtis.

"I don't know what to tell you," Amanda said.

"Does God ever talk to you?"

"In an audible voice?"

"Yes."

"No."

Curtis wanted a resounding, yes. No, only brought forth more doubt and fear; and enough fear was had at his job, that he had almost become immune to feeling much of anything, at all.

"Let's cast all this worry aside, at least tonight." A tender kiss, and Amanda guided Curtis to the bedroom.

Deep intimacy.

That fervid embrace between husband and wife brought much needed physical healing to their exhausted, sweat covered bodies. It was the spiritual side, Curtis and Amanda now had to contend with.

"You're everything to be, Curtis." Amanda cuddled up, under his arm.

Sleep then washed over and caressed her away.

Curtis inhaled the sweet aroma of her hair and felt her subtle breath tickle his chest.

Is there even a bible in this house? he thought and glanced over at the half-opened window.

A midnight moon, blue in hue, shined bright in twilight splendor.

11

A lemon-yellow sun cut sharply through the multi-colored stain glass window at Northside Baptist Church like intense sabers of broken light that began to play miss-happen tricks upon Heather Stockton.

Every few seconds, she caught slight glimpses of tiny air-borne orbs that seemed to dance within that lemon-yellow sun which made the implication of how small the human race really is drown out the heavy sound of approaching footsteps.

They came from behind.

"Ready?"

Mitch Taylor touched her shoulder.

Heather flinched, short of breath. "You scared me."

"Sorry," Mitch said. "I didn't mean to." He asked again, "Ready?"

Heather followed him to his office.

It was clean, and freshly vacuumed from just yesterday, when Mitch had counseled, newly divorced and single, Mrs. Adams, and said how God would forgive the severing of her twenty-year marriage vow to Mr. Adams—just as God would surly forgive him for his sneaky, philandering ways.

Now it was Heather Stockton's turn to seek pastoral guidance.

She sat.

Mitch smiled. "What's the problem?"

"This is difficult." Heather's eyes darted down because of what was about to be purged from her dark past.

Some details were not touched upon because some details were just too much in the realm of carnal sin—even for Mitch Taylor—Northside Baptist's newly appointed pastor to a select few, amidst the fifty thousand souls who comprised the vast desert sand community in Hobbs, New Mexico.

Heather had been careful about not saying too much about what had been done in college, but had said enough for Mitch to understand. He told her that God remembers her sin no more—far as the east is to the west.

"Which is about as far as one's sin can get."

"Are you sure?" How Heather felt sure didn't balance the line of cleansed forgiveness—be it east or west, or anywhere in between.

"Do you have faith in what Christ did on the cross is enough for your salvation?"

Tears were rising.

"Yes," Heather said.

"Have you confessed to God, what you confessed to me?"

Heather nodded. She was too choked up at the moment to speak.

Mitch smiled. "Then all's forgiven, Heather."

"All?" Her voice had returned and resonated with the air of a little girl who sought the loving embrace of a father.

"God does not remember that night, back when you were in college, and what happened."

"Really thought I had crossed some line of no return." Heather shivered. "Something that could not be forgiven."

"Only one sin is unforgiveable." Right then, Mitch wished his tongue had been frozen because he knew what question would be shot back. He braced himself.

"What, one sin?" Heather asked. Anyone would, if salvation of any kind was of earnest concern; but most don't study enough vested interest in the bible to find out exactly what that one sin actually is. Mitch had, though. He slowly said—"Blaspheming, the Holy Spirit. That's the only sin, unforgiveable, Heather."

"What's blaspheming, the Holy Spirit?"

To approach the topic without utmost reverence, would be like handling high explosives near a blazing fire—because what Mitch was about to explain, from intense study—this set sin in high-handed manner—severs any and all last resort from the Holy Spirit. Once that happens, no longer is there any pricking of conscience. Mitch explained further—"When someone truly blasphemes, the Holy Spirit, that person, whoever they are, cares less about their actions. Let alone, sin. They travel down a path of ill repute, with no way, spiritual speaking, of obtaining God' grace, anymore."

"Even if they ask for forgiveness?"

"That's just it Heather, that person won't ask for forgiveness, and will go through life with heavy indifference toward all that pertains to holiness and God."

"Even church?"

"Especially church."

"So, everyone against God and going to church has blasphemed, the Holy Spirit?"

"Those are mostly people who have had false doctrine drilled into them and firmly believe God is some tyrant, ready to strike them down. Someone who truly blasphemes, the Holy Spirit is one who once walked in a true relationship with God then turns completely away from that once true relationship, and won't ever return."

"How do you know so much about that sin?"

Mitch took as deep breath. "Because I once thought I had done just that…Blasphemed, the Holy Spirit."

⌒

'Stay put,' the monster said. 'Hear me, stay put, Mitch.' His stepfather then lurched—'Little late comin' in.' The monster now had Mitch's mother by the throat, soon as she came through the door. 'Well, Tab got an answer for what y'r late?' The monster stood tall, firm and muscle strong.

Tabitha's reply barely met air. 'Stop Henry…You're choking me.'

'Dat's the point. Choke ya plum crazy so ya'll come home at a decent hour.' The monster's tightening grip squeezed down harder.

This violent onslaught, forced Mitch up. Now he stood tall, firm. Muscle strong wouldn't come for another two years.

'Stay away from my mother, you—" Foul, insulting word.

The monster turned from Tabitha. "W'atchaya call me, ya little worm?' The monster's tightening grip released her.

She cried—'Stay away from my son!'

The monster now had that tightening grip around Mitch's throat.

Veins bulged and pulsed with every breath. Mitch was near close to total black out but was somehow able to land a swift, sudden kick to the groin.

The monster wailed in gut-wrenching pain and tossed Mitch aside as if he were nothing more than a tattered sheet that had been brought in from wind-battered weather.

That thing that Tabitha had married then stalked close.

Mitch lay in a corner—helpless, but far from beat. There was still stout, insistent fight left in him.

Strength had returned and all fear faded.

Cuff-to-fists.

The fight was full-on now.

Monster/Mitch/Monster/Mitch/Monster/Monster/ Mitch/Monster/Mitch.

The last punch landed squarely on the monster's jaw.

Now, the thing that claimed to be Mitch's step-father, lay in the same corner Mitch had just rose from, mere seconds ago, before the fight.

'What now?' he asked his mother.

A knock came from the front door. Tabitha answered it.

Jerry Hyde, the neighbor from down the way, stood before the threshold.

'Heard all kinds a commotion goin' on in here. Everything fine?' Nicotine clouded eyes locked hard onto the monster that lay on the floor, still out of breath. 'What da?'

———

"That's when the police were called," Mitch confirmed. "And Henry went to jail."

"For how long?"

A compromise in position had just risen. There was one factor to the whole ordeal that Mitch had purposely left out—the bible states how one's sin will finally find them out, and that long-ago sin Mitch had done, had now come to collect.

"Henry didn't actually go to trial."

"Why?"

Mitch finally confessed—"Because I killed, Henry."

Heather was taken aback. Here was Northside Baptist's newly appointed pastor in confession to murder, or so it seemed. Was there more to what Mitch had just said? Or had he done what he had confessed, killed Henry? Mitch continued—"While the monster was jailed up one night, I baked cookies…Laced with rat poison. Then when it came time to visit; don't ask me why my mom did that; but she did; anyway, when me and my mom visited, Henry…I gave him those rat-laced cookies. Kind of my own farewell-peace-offering.

"Well, Henry ate them. Then died, two days later. The county jail just assumed it was a food poisoning.

"After I gave Henry what I gave him, the whole jail got sick. Bad sick. The type of sick, anyone would want to die from. Come to find out, the county jail had got a hold of a batch of rotted potatoes, same day I gave Henry those rat-laced cookies.

"Instead of chunking them, the cook boiled the potatoes, mashed them down, and served them. To everyone. Even warden Tipton.

"No one else but Henry died. That's when the official autopsy was done. And that's when traces of rat poison was found in Henry. And that's when warden Tipton knocked on my mom's door. And that's when I confessed to warden Tipton. I wasn't going to let my mom take the fall for something I did. So, I confessed.

"After that, and after my trial, I was found guilty, and sent off to Texas's Wentworth Boys Home."

A deep breath escaped Mitch. "So, Heather, you're past my not be as sin-checkered as you think."

"But murder," she said, "isn't, from what you said, blaspheming, the Holy Spirit." Fear rose because abortion also had been a well-hidden sin treaded upon by, Heather. "Is it," she continued. "Is murder blaspheming, the Holy Spirit?"

Mitch shook his head. "No."

"Then why did you think you blasphemed, the Holy Spirit?"

Another quagmire Mitch Taylor now had to trudge through. Too much was already in the open to shun avoidance.

He continued—"Two days after I got to Wentworth's, I got jumped and almost…Well, think you know what without me mentioning. Anyway, after that, about another two days later, in the middle of the night, while everyone slept, I went into the head; that's what's called the bathroom, and found a private place in the showers and cursed God and told Him, 'if this is what it means to be a Christian, I don't want it, anymore. And I'm not coming back. Ever. Not after how You let me and my mom get tortured by that monster, Henry. So, You can take my salvation, if that's what You call it, and cram it.' "Then do you know what I did, Heather? I spit straight up to heaven, held my arms out like I was on the cross, like Christ, and said, 'It's finished. You hear me, God? Finished. I'm finished with You, and not coming back, so don't try and woe me You…"

Mitch choked back the word. Just rehashing what happened was enough without full-on vulgarity. Besides, that word, if spoken again, would have been be like calling God, the Father that degrading insult, all over again. Something Mitch Taylor wasn't about to do—even in confessing to dear Heather Stockton, what was said.

She exhaled. "You really said all that?"

Mitch nodded. "So, I truly know the fear of having possibly blasphemed, the Holy Spirit. Because I really thought I had.

"Later that night, after I went back to my bunk, I had the worse sense of conviction I ever felt. All I could do was cry out to God, and beg His forgiveness. Took me close to twelve years, though, after that, and after graduating from seminary, to truly believe I hadn't blasphemed, the Holy Spirit."

"What finally convinced you?"

"God's word states: 'all that the Father gives Me, shall come to me, and the one who comes to Me, I will, in no way, cast out.' That verses, as well as this one, 'whoever calls upon the name of the Lord, shall be saved.' "But it took me many years to finally get to where I truly believed, God had forgiven me, for what I had said, and how I had said it."

Nothing more could be said on the subject. Mitch Taylor had covered all spiritual bases that pertained to that vile, high-handed sin against Holy Light.

Regardless, countless throes are plagued by deep despair over the fear of having possibly blasphemed, the Holy Spirit, and committed, the unpardonable sin.

The reason for such fear usually is heavy demonic oppression.

Someone in that state suddenly finds conduct once not so hard to resist, a down-right incessant compulsion that cannot be stopped until fulfilled.

Thus begins a vicious cycle of torturous bondage, unbroken until God, the Father grants total deliverance through complete and steadfast faith in, Christ Jesus.

Then there's full-on demonic possession where a demon actually enters the fleshly body of a human host by means of the mind where the demon can then use the human host to commit heinous acts of violence upon other humans. But the soul reason for either demonic oppression or full-on possession is to get whichever human broken down so spiritually that that human becomes weak in will power and is then susceptible in temptation to blaspheming, the Holy Spirit.

Mitch explained that, all of that to, Heather; he also added, "So many people have come to me, worried they have blasphemed, the Holy Spirit, until I tell them my own testimony. Then it's a whole lot of biblical counseling and scripture." He glanced at the clock. "Well, Heather, time's up. But don't worry about our talk. I'm very much like a lawyer. Sworn to privacy."

"Thanks," Heather said. "You helped, more than you know." She suddenly fell silent.

"What is it?"

Heather breathed. "Murder isn't, the unpardonable sin?"

Mitch knew what lay heavy upon her. "No, murder is not, the unpardonable sin. Either in cold blood…Or abortion. Both are forgivable, Heather."

She couldn't believe how Mitch knew exactly what concern had brought forth such trepidation in sin. She was truly glad for knowing the resound truth, that she was now forgiven and no longer marked in shame from the sins of her youthful past.

After goodbyes said, Heather left the office and sensed God's Holy forgiveness pour down and wash over.

Now back behind his desk, Mitch Taylor began to pray for guidance for next week's carefully noted sermon.

It would scale forgiveness.

12

Hell's Gates.

Lucifer: Have you broken the Harris household, yet?

Azur: In time.

Lucifer: Time is something I don't have. I want the Harris household broken and lost with no way of turning back. Do you hear me?

Azur: I've done all I know.

Lucifer: Infect the child's dreams. Place fear deep inside.

Azur: I don't know if that will suffice. Miguel has shown himself to the child. Jessica, I believe her name is.

Lucifer: I know the child's name, Azur. Far as Miguel, engage in battle with him. Get inside his head.

Azur: Should full concentration be placed upon, Jessica. Or, Miguel.

Lucifer: Weaken first, Miguel. Then Jessica will have no true heavenly protection.

Azur: What if she calls upon the name of—

Lucifer: Don't give that child that much credit. Has she or her family ever once darkened the door of a church?

Azur: No.

Lucifer: Faith comes by hearing and hearing the Word of God. That absentee Landlord wanted me, his most beautiful angel to bow down in subjection and worship those earth bound misfits. I was the one who conducted heavenly music before the mercy seat. Then God goes and creates beings a little lower than us. Us, angels, to worship those earth bound misfits. I think not. Half the time, they don't know which end is up. Do you want some earth bound misfit in subjection over you, Azur?

Azur: No.

Lucifer: However much God wants His little fleshly experiment in constant worship to Him, He must realize that those earth bound misfits don't have that kind of spiritual strength instilled in the them now, after what Adam did. God will then have to admit I was right, that to create those earth bound misfits, in the first place, was all a grave mistake, He would soon come to regret. But not to worry, Azur. Doesn't God's own word state, His mercies are new each day?

Azur: Yes.

Lucifer: He will have mercy, Azur, and welcome us back home. Just like the prodigal son. Each of us Azur is a prodigal son.

Azur: God's word also states how we lose in the end.

Another demon entered the fray.

Tuka: Cody Holt is almost broken. Should be no more than a few days, at most. If that. Mostly likely, around Thanksgiving. I have him believing he actually blasphemed, the Holy Spirit.

Lucifer: More mental institutions house more earth bound misfits in fear of that very sin, having blasphemed, the Holy Spirit. Azur?

Azur: Yes.

Lucifer: Convince Jessica she's done just that, blasphemed, the Holy Spirit.

Tuka: Concerning my assignment?

Lucifer: Bend in.

Tuka: How hard?

Lucifer: Until Cody Holt, or I should say, Chaz Spivey kills himself.

Azur: Should the same approach be taken with, Jessica?

Lucifer: Get her in a mental institution. Then the rest will follow.

Azur: The rest?

Lucifer: Once Jessica is housed up in restraints, one of her parents, Derek, or Amber, will eventually do themselves in. Then once one goes, the other will follow suit. Then when Jessica is finally release to pick up what's left of her life, she'll reflect back and think it's all her fault, her parents having killed themselves, like they did. Jessica will then be not able to handle the guilt, and do herself in, just like how her parents did. Maybe not in the same fashion, but done in, just the same, like sweet, poor, Marilyn. Remember her, sweet poor, Marilyn.

Azur and Tuka: We've got that seven year itch.

Lucifer: Then get to it. The both of you.

13

Sixty pills were carefully counted, poured into a prescription bottle labeled, Zoxin—one pill, twice daily—and slid into a paper sack, stapled shut, and handed across the counter to Derek Harris.

"There, Mr. Harris." Sandra Murray smiled, latex gloves on. This was Sandra Murray's eighth month working at Beverly Hills Pharmacy as leading pharmacist, and had developed a pleasant repertoire with all customers. "Once month's worth." Brown eyes took in Derek's appearance— shirt not ironed, slight five o'clock shadow, and this sullen air that seemed to have followed him, all the way to the counter. "You okay, Mr. Harris?"

Tip-top. Sure am. That's why I'm here for my head pills. Thoughts soon cleared.

"Yeah, sure. How have you been, Sandra?"

"Expecting." She showed latex covered hands. "The reason for these," she said. "Can't let any prescribed medication get into my bloodstream, through touch." She rubbed her stomach. "Haven't come up with a name, yet. Any suggestions, Mr. Harris?"

Sweat trickled down his armpits, but he didn't want to rush off in rudeness. "Well, Sandra, know what you're having?"

"Only two months along." She smiled. "Haven't got my first ultra-sound, yet. Next week, for sure, though."

"Ask me again when you do. Wouldn't really be fair to come up with a great name, not knowing if you're having a boy or girl."

"If I'm having a boy, what name would you give?"

"I really have to go. The bible's always a great place to look for boys names. Take care, Sandra."

"You, too, Mr. Harris. Have a blessed day."

"Will do."

Like that, Derek Harris turned, walked out of Beverly Hills Pharmacy, broke into a quick jog, back to the Lexus, got in, re-locked the door, and tore into the paper sack; then took a long, hard stare in the rear-view mirror.

What happened to me? One day, fine. The next, can't even function. It's not suppose to be this way.

How it wasn't suppose to be, was how it was. Derek Harris couldn't rationalize any of what was taking place—sudden dark moods—sudden shift in temper—sudden jimble-jamble thoughts. Not the exact path he envisioned his life on. And certainly not, staying upon. Something soon had to break and give way. Derek just hoped it wasn't his already fractured sanity.

He gazed at the prescription bottle.

Pills better work. And work well. I'm not going through this for nothing. I have a job. A family, Amber and Jessica. All is weighing strong if these little suckers get my head straight again. I'm Derek Harris, ICM Super Agent.

An elderly lady caught sight of Derek whispering to himself.

Agnes Smith stopped, walked over to the Lexus and tapped on the driver side window.

Derek rolled it down. "Yeah?"

"You were talking to no one but yourself," Agnes said. "Saw it myself. You okay? Don't really look it. Not at all."

"I'm fine," Derek said. "I was just reading aloud, the prescription directions. Thanks for the concern, though. Take care." *Leave lady. Go back, wherever you came from. Oh no, no more, please.*

"You look all strung out." Agnes leaned in. "Sure do."

"I'm not," Derek said. "But thank you, anyway. Have a nice day."

Agnes walked off but not without cell phone in hand. She didn't believe what Derek had said, and took it upon herself to phone in a complaint to the Beverly Hills Police, about a man in a Lexus, in the Beverly Hills Pharmacy parking lot that seemed, Agnes voiced—"All strung out. Yes, officer. Just sitting in that Lexus of his. Talking to himself. Bet that

Lexus isn't even his. Bet it's stolen. Where? Like I already said, the Beverly Hills Pharmacy. Yes, that's where. Hurry, too. Guy looks up and ready to detonate. Okay, I'll wait. Yes, officer, I understand. You need me here as witness. I'll wait. Yes, I'll wait."

Five minutes later, two black and white cruisers swarmed the scene.

What now, Derek thought, and watched two uniformed Beverly Hills police officers make their way to the Lexus.

All the while, safe in her room, Jessica talked and played with, Miguel.

The demon, Azur stealthily lurked.

14

"If God was here before everything, where did God come from?"

Miguel smiled. "I can't answer that for you, Jessica. Something's even I haven't full knowledge of."

"But you're an angel."

"Being an angel doesn't grant me anymore insight on something's then you, Jessica."

"That's not fair."

Miguel smiled again. "But I believe I can give you an answer why I don't have all the answers."

"Tell me, Miguel."

He explained that once one is given much knowledge, much responsibility is required in much greater measure then if never knowing that which was sought. For once knowledge is digested to heart, that knowledge becomes a part of whoever obtained it; and if not carefully guarded, such newly obtained knowledge, if not wisely used for the betterment of good, will inevitably destroy whoever sought to obtain it.

"And," Miguel explained further, "if I knew everything, *I would* be, God."

"Bet you're glad you're not, huh?"

"Yes, Jessica, I'm glad I'm not, God."

"Would still be pretty neat, though, to be Him, for a while. Like when I take my tests at school. Being, God would come in pretty handy, then. Hey, speaking of school, think I'll get to second grade? Tell the truth. Don't lie. Just because we're such good friends."

"You'll do just fine, Jessica."

"How you know for sure?"

"I've been watching over you."

"My guardian angel?"

"That's me. You're guardian angel. Just to let you know, Jessica, I can't lie."

"Bet any lawyer would want you on the stand." She reached to hug Miguel; but before her arms clasped tight—the fallen angel, Azur materialized.

The demon had watched and heard all said from the far left corner of the room. Only, Azur didn't look evil, nor demonic. His false façade was nothing more than that of an ordinary, average man.

"I could show you how to lie, Miguel. Sure could."

"Is that God, Miguel?" Jessica flashed her missing-front-tooth smile.

Demonic laughter. "Oh, child, that almost make me want to wave the white flag." Azur turned to, Miguel. "You know I won't do that, though, don't you? Because I have a job to do."

Before Miguel could reply, Jessica asked, "What job?"

Miguel warned, "Don't talk to him anymore, Jessica… Please, don't." She hid behind the heavenly angel's back. Fear had risen.

"What if she wants to? You can't do anything about that. Freewill, remember. The child can speak whomever she sees fit. Isn't that right, dear child?" Azur took a step forward. "Do you know what job I'm here for, Jessica? It's okay, you can ask me. I'm an angel, too."

Curiosity had gotten the very best of her; she had to ask, "What job?"

"You dear, child." Satanic grin. "Yes, you, Jessica, you're my job. The job I'm here to do."

"Enough," Miguel said. "Leave."

Azur turned—"I've had just about enough of you and your mouth!"

"You need to be spanked," Jessica spout. "You're a bad man."

"Child, I'm no man."

Miguel pleaded, "Jessica, please stay quite. I'll handle this."

"Handle nothing, you will." Azur slapped his hand tight around Miguel's mouth, then morphed into his true demonic form.

A demon now stood before Jessica. She cried—"God, where are you?" Silence. "You're not there, are you, God?" Hot tears streamed down.

Azur finally saw the opening needed to get to Jessica.

"Say that again, child, what you just said."

Being only six, Jessica didn't know what was transpiring. She slowly said—"You're not there are you, God?"

Azur grinned. "You've done it now, child."

"Done what?" Jessica sniffled back tears.

"Blasphemed, the Holy Spirit." Satanic lie. "Yes, you have, Jessica, blasphemed, the Holy Spirit. So sad, you have done what you just did. Yes, so sad."

Miguel broke free from Azur's grip. "Don't listen to him, Jessica." The angel slumped down, void of all energy. Just the touch from Azur had sent shocking current throughout— as if being hit by high voltage.

"I don't know who to listen to, anymore." Tears ran in a free-fall-stream down trembling cheeks, and Jessica ran to the closet, hand on knob. Azur stopped her.

"You can't run from this, child. What you just said, has sent your eternal soul to hell."

"But I'm just six!" Jessica couldn't stop the flow of tears that still ran down her cheeks like baptismal drops of hot rain.

"Only six, huh," Azur cackled. "How unfortunate for you. And you do know that six is the number of man, and the number of the Beast."

"No, I didn't," Jessica cried. She hit knees and began to pray.

"Well," Azur said, "you do now."

Miguel sluggishly got to his feet, shook off the demonic assault, and quickly stepped forth. "Enough, Azur. Leave Jessica alone." She was still in prayer.

The demon turned. "I've had enough of your sharp tongue, Miguel." Azur lunged—ready to inflict more spiritual damage.

Then—Holy light engulfed the room and surrounded Jessica in a hedge of divine protection. She was shielded from any further demonic assault.

Christ then stepped forth. He graciously walked over and told Jessica—"You did not do what that demon said."

"He said he was an angel."

Holy smile. "Azur lied."

The demon was now far away, near the window. "Son of the most High, want do You want with me." There was no reply, only silence. Azur's lips had just been sewn shut.

Miguel sauntered passed and asked Christ, "How?"

The Savior smiled, "Jessica prayed Me here." He placed His hand upon her shoulder. "Sleepy, aren't you?"

Tiny yawn. "A little." She flashed her missing-front-tooth smile.

Christ swiftly carried her over to her bed. "Go ahead and sleep." He gently kissed her forehead, and that pinkish scar, above her left eye, was now and forever healed. She now lay in peaceful splendor.

Christ turned—"What has taken place in this room, isn't over. It's just begun, Miguel."

"But, Lord," the angel said. "Jessica sleeps. And the demon is silent."

Christ replied—"It's just begun, Miguel."

The smell of pungent sulfur soon gripped the room.

Flames followed the step of cloven hooves.

"That's right, it's just begun," Lucifer spat. "You're angel there, broke the rules, and showed himself and influenced that dirt monkey on the bed." Demonic step forward.

Christ came between.

"Jessica has not reached the age of accountability."

"What does that have to do with anything?"

"Not being of the age of accountability, Jessica is not held responsible for anything spoken to her by, Miguel. Not that he was trying to ruin her faith. Not like how your fallen angel was."

"You and your rules." Lucifer burned hot with seething hatred.

"I say nothing I do not hear My heavenly Father say."

"Back to that again?" Satanic eyes stared. "Still see your heel is bruised."

"As if your head." Christ sat beside, Jessica. "No longer will you have hold of this child."

Azur's lips were finally free.

The demon cautiously stepped forth.

"I no longer want to do this. I no longer want to torment the child."

Lucifer came close. "How dare you pull this! In front of me, no less!"

Azur turned to, Christ. "Tell the Father I no longer want to be this way. Tell the Father, I beg for mercy."

Christ walked to the window. It opened.

Heavenly light hit Azur.

The demon twitched, convulsed, and slithered about—as if being hit again and again by electric fire. The heavenly light had completely consumed the demon. Azur had been incinerated to absolute nothing.

Smoldering ashes lay on the floor. Putrid smoke rose to the ceiling.

A crisp, clean fall breeze then blew in and carried Azur's ashes off—out the open window, up to eternal ether—where the heavenly Father patiently waited with an urn, to keep the demon's ashes sealed tight until Judgment Day, at the Great White Throne.

The window shut.

Christ told Miguel—"Now it's over."

Lucifer spat—"For now."

"You lose in the end," Miguel said. "Finally accept that."

Christ placed His hand upon the angel. "No more words spoken to the Son of the Morning Star."

The heavenly light that had just incinerated Azur, filled the whole room and pushed back Lucifer. There was no trace evidence that the fallen angel had even been there. Jessica and her room smelled freshly washed and cleansed.

She would have no memory of the hell-sent demon that had surfaced.

Her eyes slowly fluttered open, and her tiny hand touched her eyebrow. "My scar feels different." Her missing-front-tooth smile lit up the room.

Christ smiled back. "Because it is."

Miguel was over at the tea set, perfectly spread out upon the table. The tea set had been bought for Jessica on her fifth birthday, as had an over-sized Teddy bear, lovingly nicknamed, Mr. Teddy. The stuffed Teddy bear sat in a small rocking chair with a small, removable hand-held mirror in its paw. Nothing had moved at all during the whole demonic attack.

Miguel gingerly removed the mirror from Mr. Teddy's paw and walked over to Jessica. "Look."

"It's gone," Jessica said. "My scar. It's gone."

Christ smiled. "How'd that happen?"

"You," Jessica smiled. "You did that." She paused for a moment then asked, "If I fill up my bathtub, think you could walk on water again?" Christ smiled. Jessica wasn't done. "Wait, why not spend the night then go to school with me for Show-N-Tell." She then whispered, "Remember what you did with that little boy's fish?" Christ lovingly nodded. "Think you could do that with pizza?"

Christ's smile was warm and soft. "Now, who told you that?"

Jessica pointed to, Miguel. "Him. He told me a lot about You. You and, God."

Christ turned to the angel. "Keep ministering to her."

"Yes, Lord."

From downstairs, Derek's voice echoed. He began to tell Amber, in a swift, sudden ramble, what had happened in the Beverly Hills Pharmacy parking lot, and how Agnes Smith had phoned the police, and how cuffs were drawn and Derek nearly arrested and tossed in the back of a waiting police cruiser.

Christ told Jessica, "I have to go, now."

"Really?"

Christ smiled. "I won't be far away."

"Promise?" Missing-front-tooth smile.

"I promise, Jessica." The Savior then made *His* own left front tooth disappear, smiled back, and was up, off the bed and walking away.

She laughed, watched Him continue to walk away, only to call back out—"Wait!"

Christ turned, walked back and knelt down. "Yes."

"Miguel told me about this thing called being, Saved. How do *I* get Saved?"

"You are Saved, Jessica." Christ kissed her cheek. The Holy Savior knew her faith would never falter, nor waiver. He turned to, Miguel. "Keep ministering to her."

"Yes, Lord." The angel then watched Christ ascent back up to heaven.

"Neat," Jessica announced. "How did He do that?"

Miguel smiled. "One day, you'll know."

Once again, Derek's swift, sudden ramble, filtered up into the room and surrounded, Jessica. There was no mistaking it this time. Jessica knew her daddy was home.

She left Miguel standing alone, raced downstairs and told everything—except for the demon. What was said, held Derek and Amber in total disbelief.

15

Not finding a bible anywhere had Curtis Paxton on edge. He could have sworn there was at least one, somewhere—anywhere. But there wasn't. Not even in the tightly packed boxes that had remained untouched in the spare, dust-laden attic from the wedding, fifteen-years ago, gifts given by friends and family.

Still, no bible. None of that mattered now.

Curtis walked through the door at Grace Christian Bookstore, off Fairfax.

"Can I help you?" asked a sales clerk. The name, Neil in bold, black letters was stenciled across the young man's nametag.

"Actually, you can, Neil," Curtis said. "I'm looking for a bible." He scanned the rows of shelves that held different translations of the Holy text—The Amplified; The Living Bible; The Message; New American Standard; New King James; and of course, the King James version, itself—reliable, and without any questionable modern day interpretation inserted into the Holy text.

Curtis's hand fell upon, The Message.

"Stay away from that one, Sir," Neil cautioned. "It's mostly American slang, more than anything else." He put The Message back on the shelve.

"Why carry it, then?"

"Not my store," Neil said. "If it were, The Message wouldn't be carried."

Lyrics, *Don't push me cuss I'm close to the edge; I'm tryin' not to lose my head,* from Grandmaster Flash's famous Eighties opus, The Message, filled Curtis's thoughts.

"Have you accepted Christ?" Neil asked.

Grandmaster Flash and his Brooklyn rap about life in New York City and the perils that await all, fresh off the bus, faded. "What?" Curtis said.

Neil smiled. "Have you accepted Christ?"

"No. I don't think so."

"Would you like to?"

"How?"

Neil guided Curtis over to an out-of-the-way corner, in back, reserved for private reading.

They both sat, and Neil explained—"Once you know you're a sinner, simply pray to God, in the name of Christ, ask for forgiveness for the sins you've done, then ask Christ into your heart, to be your saving Savior and guide your life. Here, if you like, I can help you pray."

Really think a simple prayer, like that will bring forth eternal salvation, Curtis? You're smarter than that.

Curtis pulled back. "Did you hear that?"

"Hear what?"

"That voice."

"What voice?"

Curtis told exactly what had been whispered into his ear. Strangely enough, Neil remained unfazed. He knew what had happened, and swiftly laid hands on Curtis and prayed, "Heavenly Father, in the name of your Son, Christ Jesus, I bind this oppressive demonic spirit."

That demonic spirit, which had so briefly brought forth oppression—vanished. The hellish phantasm no longer whispered doubt and unbelief. Simple faith in prayer, in the name of Christ Jesus, demonstrated by Neil—had vanquished any and all stock trace of what had once surrounded Curtis.

He still couldn't move; but knew something had happened—something profound and unexplainable. The English lexicon held no word to accurately describe what had suddenly, and without warning, transpired and took place. What words truly could? None that Curtis could conjure. Even "miracle" fell far and short in proper description.

All he knew to ask, "Was that really a demon?"

"Yes, it was, Curtis."

"But why now, and why me?"

"Because you're finally ready to claim Christ as your Savior. And that demon sensed it and tried to stop it."

"How and what should I pray?"

Heads bowed, and eyes shut, this heartfelt prayer filled the air, "Christ Jesus, I know I am a sinner. Not only against You, but also, God, the Father. I humbly come before you now and graciously ask for forgiveness of my sins. Past, present, and future, and to be cleansed in your Holy blood, Christ Jesus. Amen. And amen."

Exhaustion pulsed, and Curtis finally raised his head. "I'm tired."

"Considering what came against you," Neil said, "I can see why."

"I don't feel anything, though. Sure God heard my prayer?"

"Yes," Neil confirmed. "God, heard. But remember: a person walks by faith, not sight." Neil explained further, "Times *will* come where it seems God can't be found."

A familiar voice came from behind.

"Thought that was your car, I saw in the parking lot." Ryan Garrett surveyed where he was, and didn't know, until right then, he was standing in a Christian bookstore. He knelt down and met Paxton, eye to eye. "Just why are you here?"

Curtis said he had just accepted Christ and also told of the quick, but memorable demonic attack.

"You been smoking old news print, or what?" Ryan laughed.

"I heard a demon," Curtis said, "whisper in my ear, like I said. And yes, I accepted, Christ."

Neil turned to Ryan. "Have you?"

"Have I what?"

"Accepted, Christ?" Neil asked.

Curtis also asked, "Well, have you?"

Silence swirled. Ryan just stood there. The question had never once been directed toward him. Sure, he had gone to church, or more to the point, been forced to by his parents when Ryan Garrett was young, impressionable, and full of glided, adolescent angst. Ryan could, back then, pour on charm and polite manner in conduct, so no one was wiser, or even suspected, he hadn't ever hit knees and cried out to Christ for salvation—even though no submersion in the baptismal tank had ever occurred. At least not in the eyes of the congregation at Four Corners Gospel Church.

Back home had been different.

One night, while bubble-bath-slathered in the tub, Ryan—because he had seen it, more than once—took it upon himself to do exactly what he had seen time and again at Four Corners Gospel Church and had baptized himself there that night in the tub.

What Ryan didn't know was that God had taken into account that "spur of the moment" choice and had placed two angels around, to watch over and protect. Might very well explain how things simply just worked out for him. Whatever Ryan went after, he accomplished—until just recently. Here lately, a great and unseen weight bore down with vice-tight pressure. Ryan was under Holy Spirit conviction. Only he didn't know it. But he explained, best he could, what he had been going through and how he felt for weeks past.

"Holy Spirit conviction," Neil confirmed. "That's exactly what you've been feeling. But you're at the right place to answer that conviction. Are you ready?"

Ryan had never heard it put so blunt. Mostly what flooded his recollection of church was a preacher behind a podium, bible open, and the congregation, half asleep— dressed in Sunday best. Not once had there ever been mention of Holy Spirit conviction—much less demonic oppression. This was all new—that demons lurked, here upon the earth to oppress and regrettably, possess most of the human race before Christ's return upon horseback with a shout.

Neil continued to minister the gospel.

Holy Spirit conviction pressed in even harder.

Ryan slightly wobbled, back-forth/back-forth.

No more denying what Neil preached—for each word spoken, struck with spiritual clarity that resonated deep within Ryan Garrett's soul. His inner most being had been rocked and shook to its very core.

Ryan still slightly wobbled—back-forth/back-forth. Neil and Curtis were there and eased him down in a chair.

He slumped, eyes blinking fast—as if hooked up to electromagnetic meters that registered hidden thoughts that had been stowed deep down within the vast recesses of a newly awakened mind.

Amy Rodgers, another Grace Christian Books employee, rushed up, and turned to Neil. "He okay?"

"Yeah," Neil said. "He's just a little—"

"Spooked," Ryan finally said, heavy pant. "Got any water?" Curtis stood, speechless.

Amy ran to the storeroom; then ran back. "Here," she said. "Here's the water."

"Thanks." Ryan downed the water then looked at, Curtis. "You really accepted, Christ?"

"I did, Ryan."

"Are *you* ready to, as well?" Neil asked.

Holy Spirit conviction pressed down hard again.

This time, Ryan answered the call, and Neil guided him, as he had with Curtis, into what has become known as, The Sinner's Prayer unto Salvation.

Eyes open, Ryan raised his head. "I don't feel any different."

"The feeling you're talking about," Amy said, "doesn't happen for everyone."

"How will I know God even answered my prayer, let alone saved me?"

Neil explained, how he had to Curtis, about walking by faith, not sight.

"God doesn't move on anything but faith. When you're faith is properly anchored in Christ, God does amazing things, and will open doors, only He can. And prayers get answered without effort." Neil added, "When faith in

Christ is anchored strong with what He did on the cross, your relationship with God, the Father will blossom into a lovingly relationship."

Ryan needed the word of God. So did, Curtis.

Neil guided them back over to the bible section.

Amy was there, King James, in hand. "Here." She gave Curtis and Ryan the bibles. "No charge. Not with the angels rejoicing."

Neil explained—"Whenever one truly comes to Christ, angels in heaven rejoice over the confession of sins in repentance. Which is what you both did. So, the angels are rejoicing."

This was all too much to grasp—let alone take in. What, with the confession of sins unto salvation, and angels rejoicing because of such.

Exodus from a spiritual wilderness had just been graciously granted to Curtis and Ryan.

Neil handed his card to them both. "If either of you need to talk, or have questions, which will happen, call."

Ryan nodded. "I'll keep that in mind."

"So will I," Curtis agreed.

After goodbyes said, Curtis and Ryan, with bibles in tow, left Grace Christian Books and headed for their parked cars.

Intense biblical study was high on agenda.

16

Regret teased.

Ever since not having called Jim Jackson back—Hollywood's go-to man when dirt and shady behavior needed to be confirmed and later, swept under the rug—to do the "right" thing had just about punch drunk Tracy Powers into better judgment. All that consumed her—since Derek Harris left the office that day before his appointment with Dr. O'Connor—was setting things right. Tracy had to.

Should've kept my mouth shut. Then I wouldn't be here.

She stood before a dingy wooden door at the Winslow Apartments in the Valley—a place where Hollywood glitz and glamour faded far from camera flashes and fan frenzy at movie premieres.

The only camera flashes that ever really popped at the Winslow Apartments were when police and CSI showed at a crime scene. Fan Frenzy? If die hard drug fiends in search of a junk-sick-score solidified red carpet fans, then the

Winslow Apartments constituted the life teens-turn-run away hop cross-country buses to find. That's the type of life that has, and always will surround the Winslow Apartments.

Sick as it was, Jim Jackson loved that kind of life. Said it gave him an edge to his work, to squalor in and around such vulgar settings.

One reason Jim Jackson called the Winslow Apartments home: young girls that strolled outside, dusk till dawn, for money made from their used and abused bodies. Jim Jackson also jobbed the skin trade. Aside from P.I. gigs— the thirty-billion dollar a year porno industry—also paid the bills, in full.

Yes, Jim Jackson used his squat of an apartment to spy out the window; and later, approach young girls and lure them into the lie of easy money made, to afford a better life than the one they had just run from.

What Jim never did mention: loss of moral integrity, black and blue beatings, drug addiction, and a slew of STDs—transmitted in bacterial and virus infection from man/woman/ woman/man/woman, and back to man. Sometimes even children. Sad as it is, it happens.

But the most solid reason Jim Jackson called the Winslow Apartments home was because it was in the heart of the Valley where ill-gains were bore off the backs of those lured into pornographic deeds by men of lurid means and whose bottom line never fell short of the highly worshiped and sought after, American dollar.

Tracy finally gave a firm knock and took a step back.
Jim answered the door.

"Yeah?"

"I want it called off, Jim."

"What called off?"

"Chaz Spivey. I no longer need your services rendered, in that matter."

"Wait a minute—"

"You wait a minute," Tracy said. "No payment's been paid. So, drop it. I mean it, Jim."

"You called me, remember?"

"Now I say, call it off."

"Seemed real tore up about this, over the phone."

"Well, I'm not anymore. So, call it off." Tracy turned to leave when—Xavier Torrez peered over Jim's shoulder.

"Problem, Jim?" Xavier was Jim's source to all things pornographic. It had been that way since Xavier had gotten Heather Stockton up in that mansion, deep in the Hollywood hills, that night. And since that night, Xavier Torrez and Jim Jackson worked in a sick-pair partnership and supplied secret money men—naïve, ingenuous fresh faced virgin girls from the Valley, and anywhere in between—for sex trade sin on film.

Tracy stepped back.

Something about Xavier Torrez put chills deep inside. To stick around and find out exactly what caused such feelings to rise, didn't sit well. That, and the smell that suddenly

128

rose. The odor parlayed somewhere between rancid and foul. So goes it with heroin. Which Xavier partook each day—needle to vein.

Drug-fueled eyes fluttered heavy, and Xavier—mumbling something incoherent—sunk away from Jim.

"Don't mind, Xavier. He's harmless. Really he is." Jim quickly added, "Wanna come in?"

Not ever! Tracy thought; then said, "I have to go." She wasted no time turning for the stairs.

She ran in a fit of fast-flurry steps to her car—fumbled for her keys—unlocked the Porsche's door, got in—and drove off.

At the window, Xavier had watched Tracy' every move.

Whoever that was, reminds me of Heather Stockton. I should pay her a visit. Sure should.

Jim was busy with his own words. "If Tracy thinks I'm just gonna drop it, she's all wrong. I'm not dropping anything. There could still be a big payday in it for me." Jim reached for an uncharged cell phone.

It was plugged into an AC adapter, and call roamed.

Jim waited patiently for the Editor and Chief at The National Enquirer to answer.

Xavier cared less. What still swarmed his thoughts—Heather Stockton, and just exactly where she was.

20 cc's of heroin waited in an already drawn and rigged syringe.

17

"It's true," Jessica said. "I talked with an angel. And Jesus. The other day. In my room. And they talked with me, too."

"How long, Jessica," O'Connor said, "have you been talking to this angel...and—"

"Jesus?" Jessica asked. O'Connor nodded. "Just that one time, in my room. But Miguel—"

"The angel?"

"Gee, who else?" And there came Jessica's famous missing-front-tooth smile.

Derek and Amber sat silent-still. It was hard enough coming to terms with what Jessica told them yesterday, about who spent time with her in her room—let alone swallow it down in full-belief.

Those things usually don't happen, like an angel and Jesus, Himself, appearing to a little, first grade girl and speaking of things which were spoken of, in such sure detail, about heavenly salvation and eternal life—far from this present, evil world.

The scar, though—or the healing thereof—could not be cut free from truth, no matter what vague, fancy whim filled the notion. Jessica's scar was healed, never again to appear in that slight pinkish hue, above her left eye.

She gently rubbed at it. "See, Jesus healed me. My scar isn't there, anymore."

But that didn't remove the fact that Jessica was still in front of O'Connor with her parents. Derek and Amber were in as much shock over the whole ordeal as was, O'Connor—a renowned man of science and deep study within the mind that had never lent himself ponder passed any speculative thought in sound belief upon a higher, guiding power from above.

O'Connor didn't believe in God nor the bible nor the wisdom, in verse, contained therein. In no uncertain terms, O'Connor was a die-in the-wool atheist. His faith was placed in science and all things under the microscope. Anything else was eventually tossed aside and flung upon the scrap heap—never again to be noted, even in the slightest consideration.

Until now.

"And you believe in Jesus, Jessica?"

"Who you think healed my scar, gee." She turned to Amber and Derek. "How much longer, here? I'm tired."

Derek smiled. "We just want to make sure we understand you right, Jess, that's all."

"That's right, honey," Amber said, "we just want to make sure we understand you right."

"Because you don't believe me." Jessica clasped her arms tight around her body. "But I'm telling the truth: Miguel, my guardian angel and Jesus, showed up in my room, like I said. And that's that. 'Cause I know the truth."

"Not that we don't believe you, Jessica," O'Connor said. "We just want to make sure you, didn't, somehow... Imagine, all this."

Jessica's tiredness had worn down her patience. "Where'd you get your degree, Cracker Jack Academy?"

"Jessica, apologize, right now to Dr. O'Connor." Amber was serious.

She apologized, but couldn't help whisper again, "Cracker Jack Academy."

Smiles and laughter filled the office. How Jessica had said, 'Cracker Jack Academy' again, struck everyone, down-right funny.

O'Connor took a moment to reflect, and found himself, oddly enough, at slight odds with prior beliefs—or lack thereof. Maybe there was more to the grand design than he once thought?

Maybe O'Connor was finally ready to lay aside past faith in academia, and face another fact that the formation of the earth and constellational alignment of the universe, was not, by any means—haphazard chance. There was just too much perfected perfection, for that. Which O'Connor was slowly coming around to.

He lend back from his desk, hands clasped loosely behind his head, and smiled at Jessica. "You really saw, Jesus?"

"And Miguel, don't forget, my guardian angel. Sure enough. Saw them both." Jessica didn't know nor sense, Christ behind her, in spirit. The Savior gently stroked her thick mane of sandy blonde hair.

Christ was now next to, O'Connor.

Words unheard were whispered, and O'Connor perked up, "Your fine, Jessica. Just fine." Derek and Amber were beside themselves.

The trouble it took to get Jessica out of her room because she was sure that Christ and Miguel would make another surprise return—now seemed in vain—especially with O'Connor, who, at first, didn't believe Jessica's assurance, that the angel, Miguel, and Christ, Himself, had shown—less than twenty-four hours ago, and had engaged in lengthy banter on eternal life, hereafter.

Now it was Derek and Amber who could not accept such truth. Not because they didn't want to; it just seemed impossible. In the natural, of course. But with God—all things are possible—especially when God, the Father is working within the life of a precious, little child, like Jessica.

"How can you say she's fine, Dr. O'Connor?"

Derek saw it the same as Amber. "Yeah, how can you say that?"

Jessica piped in, "Because I am." Christ patted her shoulder. This time, Jessica briefly sensed His touch; but it was more like passing goose bumps, than anything else. Regardless, undeniable Holy comfort washed over. Jessica remained calm and serene—as if nothing less than a subtle spring breeze had just passed by. She affirmed again—"I'm fine. Just like Dr. O'Connor said."

"Cracker Jack Academy," he smiled.

Missing-front-tooth smile back. "I was only kidding, Dr. O'Connor."

"I know." His attention was now focused back on, Derek. "It's you, my concern should be on."

Amber told Jessica, "C'mon sweetie, let's go wait outside."

"Okay." She stopped and glared at a painting on the far left wall. "I like your…" Christ whispered, *Jack Pollock*. Jessica repeated, "Jackson Pollock." She turned to where she had heard Christ's voice. "I could do that, just throw paint all around."

Christ smiled and returned to the Father's right hand side in heaven.

Miguel had been there too, in the office, but was told by Christ to remain near Jessica.

The door to the office closed.

Amber and Jessica were walking down the hall, having left Derek in the hands of O'Connor, to try and pry loose, whatever mental disarray remained.

In the reception area, Jessica talked with Tom Nelson.

"Nice to meet you," he told Jessica.

Missing-front-toot smile. "Nice to meet you, too. Why are you here?"

"Please, sweetie," Amber said, "that's private."

Tom smiled back. "That's okay, but yeah, it is rather private." He thought—*She looks like my daughter, Vanessa.*

She had been murdered, as had Tom Nelson's wife, Stacy—one year ago, to the day. That was why, Tom Nelson, marketing executive at Capitol Records was in patient wait to see, Dr. O'Connor.

A demon suddenly whispered—*Know why she looks like, Vanessa? Because she is, Vanessa. She's returned to you, Tom. As has, Stacy. Take a close look. Is that, or is that not, Stacy there with, Vanessa?*

Tom silently answered—*Yes.*

The demon influenced Tom—*Cancel your appointment with, Dr. O'Connor, just this once. Then go sit in your car, and follow them back home. Then get rid of the guy who stepped in and took your place, with your wife, Stacy, and daughter, Vanessa. They really weren't murdered, Tom, but ran off, like you thought. Now you've found them again. Here, at Dr. O'Connor's office.*

Total lunacy.

Tom was in no shape nor form to fight against the demon that urged on such a reprobate plan in action; only Tom didn't know it was a demon that spoke such things. Tom just took the voice that spoke in his head, as nothing more than divine inspiration from divine places because Tom, over the last few months, had moved into the mystic realm of Wicca worship and transcendental meditation—

disguised from the pit of hell by demon deities—as a deific path toward enlightened light that would eventually fuse, in profound relationship—one closer to the Great Spirit in the sky—beyond the earthly coil, Tom Nelson stagnated upon.

"Think I'll re-schedule."

"Did Jessica hurt your feelings?"

"I just remembered, I planned something else today. Here lately, I've been rather absent minded."

Yes, you have, Tom. Now go wait in your car, like I said.

Tom did and waited for the Harris family to drive home.

Miguel looked toward heaven and prayed—*Lord, place a holy hedge over the Harris family.*

Christ answered—*All is in the Father's hands.*

18

Jasmine: Thought you'd never come back.

Shane: I couldn't stay away.

Jasmine: Let's not fight, anymore.

Shane: Can you ever forgive me, Jasmine.

Jasmine: There's nothing to forgive, Shane.

Shane: Yes, there is.

Jasmine: Let's not fight, anymore.

Fade to black.

An Aquafresh commercial then filled the television screen to try and convince the American public just how much they needed whiter teeth and fresher breath for that all-important jaunt through life; if not—no dates; no marriage; no kids. Plain put—no success.

At least that's how Aquafresh targeted their whiter teeth and fresher breath campaign. Them, and the hundred other slues of carefully crafted commercials, produced and marketed by corporate CEO's that radically bombard the

American public, every viewing moment of every viewing day. Lobotomized mind crime, via Technicolor entertainment.

Cody Holt, remote in hand, turned down the volume and rolled over. Watching his image and performance in Between Teardrops—only proved to make him feel worse than he already did. The demonic, hell-sent voice hadn't let up since Cody had left Arizona, two days ago. He was now holed up in Hobbs, New Mexico at The Lamplight Motel—a dingy stay-over, outskirts tenure, frequented mostly by truckers and low-cash vagrants—as well as high school Seniors who throw drug-induced-alcohol-fueled parties, to try and vainly live out pages from the critically acclaimed Jay McInerney novel, Bright Lights, Big City.

Nothing much happens in Hobbs, New Mexico. Certainty not like that was still happening with Cody Holt.

He was in the bathroom now, door locked.

I'm losing my mind. None of this normal.

Demonic whisper—*For you, it is. This is your new normal, Cody. Oh, yeah, that's right, Chaz Spivey. Your new Hollywood name. Never really did like yourself much, did you, Cody? Of course, you didn't. I know. For I have been around you, since your birth.*

"Stop it!"

Kid me not, I won't stop. I have a job to do. And that job is you, Cody Holt. So, let me do, just that. You. My job, I'm assigned to do.

Tear-filled hazel eyes.

Stop crying! Tears won't resolve the pending issue, here. You should have given higher thought than you did before cursing God that night before the mirror. Remember? Of course you do, Cody. It's been my duty to remind you, of all you said, that night. And meant, too, don't forget that. You sure did. I was there, and heard it all. Every last word. You were rather colorful in your choice of nouns and verbs. Hey, here's a great idea: pitch what you said that night to one of those sorry-seer-sucker-suit-wearing-Hollywood-jerks. You could call that little flick: How Chaz Spivey Sent Himself to Hell. Now that's an Oscar-worthy title, if there ever was, wouldn't you say? Oh, that's right: Chaz Spivey. I almost forgot.

Fear had completely consumed him.

Had anyone heard the same, would be in the same regretful spiritual state of wishing words, taken back.

Words, like bells, once rung, echo loud and clear—never to be shushed away again. Spoken in love or malice will remain constant, forever written down in large volume books in heaven—later to be given full accountant for. Good. Or bad.

The tongue can be a soothing remedy of gentle peace or a poison fanged asp of sulking, slow death. More regret can be traced back to a bleak, spurred flash of lashed-out anger toward enemy or loved one, in a calculated scheme of devised strife. Either or, shame, regret, and guilt always soon follows thereafter—until forgiveness, through God's Holy grace, cleanses such sin away, far as the east is to the west.

Which is what Cody Holt wanted: God's holy grace to cleanse away, all that was said, that night, in the bathroom, before the mirror.

Want this to stop?

"Yes."

Then kill yourself. There really is no other call to give an answer to, than that. If not, I will bear in and hound you, until you do, guaranteed assurance of that.

"I don't want to die."

You're already dead. You died that night when you said what you did, before the mirror. You really have nothing left to live for, anyway, do you? Look where you're at, in a stank-sick motel in Hobbs, New Mexico, for nothing more than chasing some girl you knew, way back in high school.

Cody sneaked up on the mirror.

What stared back was unrecognizable. It seemed as if ten more years had been added to his once beautiful face. What Cody didn't know was that the demon had placed a sly veil of deception over those hazel eyes of his that had once burned solar bright upon the silver screen.

The demon then showed itself, flesh and blood mirage—humanlike form.

Only thing that did not resemble human form—two catlike, slit eyes.

Tuka came close. "Ready?"

Cody screamed, "Leave. Go away. Please!"

A deafening silence filled the air.

Hazel eyes slowly opened.

A man sat on the basin of a soap-scum-ringed tub, and a fungus infested shower curtain hung inside. Whether fear had finally gone, or curiosity had gotten the very best, Cody stood.

"You're just a man. This can't be. You can't be real." He touched Tuka's arm—clothed in a shirt of fine silk, as well as tailor-fit trousers that adorned the demon's false human form.

Tuka grinned. "Oh, I'm real, all right. Real as the clothes I wear." The demon asked again, "Ready to kill yourself? Time's come, Cody Holt. Yes, time's come, sure has."

"I'm not going to kill myself."

"If I did just up and leave, that wouldn't stop how you're feeling. So, really no reason to carry on, this way, like you are. Time has come for you to accept the sad enviable: you are going to hell, Cody Holt. And I'm here to take you there."

Cody now rested against the wall. "I won't kill myself."

Then—"Please get the pain over with, Cody. Please." Tuka had taken on the mirage-induced image of, Heather Stockton. False radiant beauty beamed bright and filled the bathroom. But shock of it all: while Tuka looked and sounded very much like Heather Stockton—the demon had also manipulated its whisper-thin voice behind, Cody.

Heather Stockton stands before you. Just look. Is that surly not, Heather Stockton?

"It is Cody. It's me. Really it is, Cody. It's me…Heather…Stockton." Her mirage-induced image, manipulated by the demon, Tuka—came closer and whispered, "Don't you want how you feel to end? Be over and done with?"

"Yes."

"Then kill yourself, Cody. Please. Know how much it pains me to see you, like this? All tore up inside, really not wanting to live, anymore."

"Okay."

"You will, really?"

"Yes," Cody said, panting. "I really will."

Heather Stockton's image lend in with a kiss.

Worn out and energy drained, Cody returned the kiss—only to see those catlike slit eyes in heavy stare back. Cody cried—"Enough!"

Fiery flames engulfed the mirage-induced image of Heather Stockton, and the demon Tuka returned to the image of man.

"Now that were in full-agreement, Cody Holt…Go ahead, kill yourself." Catlike slit eyes stared hard. "For if you don't, I'll make you think I'm Heather Stockton again, and instead of a kiss, who know what might happen. Ever seen, Deliverance?"

Cody couldn't speak; his mouth, dry; his tongue—sticky-thick.

"I know, you're not the type to want to make much mess. So, let me see. No. No gunshot blast anywhere on you,

Cody Holt. You love your face way too much, to do that. You love your body, too, to even consider a chest wound. Besides, there's no gun handy. But there is…Anti-freeze. Yes, anti-freeze, right there in the trunk of that fancy BMW of yours."

"Do it for me."

"This is something left for your hands alone. So, get up, out of this bathroom, go to the trunk of your BMW, sang the anti-freeze, bring it back…And drink it down."

Cody was frozen stiff. Sudden fear intensified. It raged through his juddering body like sudden high-voltage whips to his nervous system that no longer properly responded to over-active-brainwaves that were now in a heated, static-frenzy-over-ride of synapse drive. Cody's brain was over-heating.

"Move," Tuka said. "I'm sick to even look at you, anymore."

Cody couldn't move—as if all will to get up—had flickered and burned, black-out-dead.

"You've given me, no recourse, but this." Tuka shape shifted into full demon form.

Cody screamed—"This has to be a dream! I'm ready to wake up!"

Tuka moved in.

"And I'm ready for you to get this over and done with. *You are* going to kill yourself tonight."

Sudden energy came quick, and Cody was to his feet; but still nowhere ready to snuff out his life.

"Stop wasting time. Nothing will change what you said before the mirror, that night."

Cody's thoughts turned to prayer.

If you can hear me God, please forgive me. I took all my frustration out on you, that night. All my anger. All my disappointment. Please forgive me for cursing You. Please!

At the BMW, Cody unlocked the trunk and regretably snagged the blue container of Peak anti-freeze. He ambled back to Room 7.

The door shut.

"Good," Tuka said. "Now get one of this plastic sealed plastic cups, near the sink, un-cap the anti-freeze, pour, then drink."

Cody did.

The Peak went down surprisingly smooth. Not too much discomfort—other than this odd, oily metallic twang that tasted of flat Sprite and left behind, a slight burning sensation—like a mild, peppery drink that had been laced in slight lime aftertaste.

Other than that, Cody wouldn't have known it was poison.

"One more cup full," Tuka urged. "You can do it." The demon poured, and lifted the plastic cup to Cody's lips. They parted. "Now, drink up."

Instead, Cody threw up all over Tuka—green bile splatter.

The demon spat—"You should have changed your name to, Regan."

It was then Cody flung himself all over the room.

First the wall; then back to the floor; then the wall again; then the floor, once more. His body became a bruised/battered mess—and landed head first into the bathroom's mirror.

Silvered shards of broken mirror, skewered his tender forehead, and crimson gore poured down Cody's trembling face. Look of having been mortar shot in war came close in describing his bloodstained appearance.

Faint heartbeat.

Fading pulse.

Cody' life slowly began to slip away.

"See you in hell, Cody Holt." Tuka vanished and left Cody on the floor.

All was not lost, though.

So much ruckus had been made, that the neighboring tenant, Alice Walker, drowning her sorrows in a fifth of Jack Daniels over a broken heart from the recent break up from her boyfriend, Keith Stipe, stumbled, while the demon said a final goodbye to Cody, to the Lamplight's main office, woke the night auditor, Aaron Fuentes, and said all what was heard, mostly cries of, 'I'm ready to wake up', and the sound of the mirror shattering, shortly thereafter.

"Better check it out, then," Aaron said.

Alice slurred, "I'm comin' with."

"Yeah," Aaron agreed, "I probably'll need a witness." He snagged the master key, and he and Alice rushed to Room 7 and opened the door.

Cody Holt still lay on the floor.

A foul stench of vomit rose.

Aaron backed up.

So did Alice.

She then saw the container of Peak anti-freeze on the table. She was sobering up, quick.

"I think he tried to kill himself."

While Aaron phoned for an ambulance, Alice glanced over and noticed that no sound resonated from the TV. The sound was completely off.

Vanilla Sky filled the screen, and Cameron Diaz mouthed—Wake up, man!

19

Darkness soon morphed and exploded into kaleidoscopic brilliance—a multicolored dimensional tunnel that swallowed Cody Holt whole and lifted his spirit up toward twilight, far from where his lifeless body still lay—in the same room, on the same floor—there, at The Lamplight Motel, and where Aaron Fuentes and Alice Walker still waited, as well—in the same room, and paced the same floor for paramedics to arrive and try and resuscitate Cody Holt's now lifeless body.

But that was all behind him now.

What waited beyond time and space, out of mortal man's feeble attempt to reach was a wide and foreboding gulf—on one side, heaven; on the other, hell.

Kaleidoscopic brilliance and that multicolored dimensional tunnel soon faded. Cody Holt now found himself on the burning side of hell. Screams from lost souls overflowed in a torrid sea of unquenched agony.

Shrilled voices screamed out as molten lava waves crashed down upon each soul, spiritually intertwined and locked eternally tight together.

Tuka waited.

"Told you I would see you here."

A burning image flickered bright.

A man reached down into the flames and lifted up, by the burnt scalp, the head of another lost soul. The man looked and dunked the burning head back into the flames; then pulled up another head.

"Where is he?"

Demonic laughter.

"Where's who."

The man cried, "The preacher who told me I was okay! Not to worry! That I was on my way to heaven!"

"Probably somewhere in those flames." Demonic laughter. "Keep looking." Tuka turned to Cody. "Your turn."

His mouth opened but no sound resonated. It seemed as if any ability to speak had been severed clean. But that didn't stop the flames from reaching out and coming.

An unseen wall of kinetic energy kept Cody Holt locked solid to where he still stood. Nothing else could be done but to except the blazing, eternal fate that now burned high and bright.

"I've waited patiently for this." Tuka clawed out for Cody.

Suddenly, the flames receded back, and Christ appeared.

The demon Tuka jerked away from the Savior.

"Hell is not Cody Holt's eternal fate. He is to come with me." Christ reached for Cody, and he collapsed into the arms of the Savior and was guided out and up from hell, into heaven and the Holy Court of Divine Justice.

Two books lay open. One: The Book of Life. The other: The Book of Repented Prayers.

A team of angels were also present. So was Lucifer. Son of the Morning Star waited with baited breath to see the outcome, where Cody Holt's eternal soul would reside. How Lucifer saw it; no other place but hell was meant for Cody Holt. How could it not? Not after what was said that night before the mirror, fourteen-some-odd-years back.

"Or was it fifteen, Cody?" Lucifer turned to Christ. "He can't remember. Just look at him. All wounded and confused. So, am I. Why was I even summoned here? Not like that dirt monkey there is, Job. You tell me: why was I summoned here? And why are You, Son of the Most High, defending him?"

"Because all is forgiven." Christ touched the Book of Life. Cody Holt's name was written therein. "Hell is not Cody Holt's eternal home." The team of angels closed in close.

Lucifer saw no marked sin written down next to Cody Holt's name. It was as if he had walked a perfect, sinless life upon earth's spiritually tainted soil after Adam and Eve brought forth knowledge of good and evil to all new born infants to be, engrained deep within genetic DNA—action in deeds of defiant disobedience against the Father, because of the Fall.

"What was said *cannot* be forgiven," Lucifer spat. "Not how Cody said it, and meant it. How could that be forgiven, Son of the Most High? How can blaspheming, the Holy Spirit be forgiven?"

Christ said, "For Cody Holt did not do what you so vehemently claim."

"Prove it!" Lucifer burned white-hot in unbelief.

Christ opened the Book of Repented Prayers and showed Lucifer were Cody Holt had silently, before ingesting the anti-freeze, cried out to the Father for forgiveness of what was said that night, before the mirror.

Christ placed his arm around Cody. "Cody Holt is now a child of My, Father. And now, My brother. He is none of yours, anymore, Son of the Morning Star. Cody Holt and his sins have forever been cleansed, in the blood of My sacrifice, upon the cross at Calvary." Christ commanded Lucifer, "Now leave, for Cody Holt's mansion now lies here, with me. His bed will nevermore be within the burning flames of Sheol. Amen."

Lucifer spat, "We'll see," and vanished to toil the earth, once more, to search out unsuspecting souls—as to devour them like a roaring lion.

Christ turned to Cody. "Follow me."

Cody did.

20

Rocks and pebbles gleamed bright in prismatic splendor at the bottom of a cool running brook that streamed out across a vast green pasture, where sparrows flew and sang springtime songs while white-spotted fawns gracefully played among humming bird flocks and butterfly swarms. It was a gentle feathered flight amidst Monarch orange, dusted grace.

Tranquility surrounded Cody as he sat there with, Christ.

"What question hangs over you?" the Savior asked.

"You know."

"Maybe I chose not to." Christ placed his hand upon Cody's shoulder. "Tell me. It's okay."

"I was sure I had crossed over some unseen line, that night, before the mirror. That's what I read in the Gospel of Matthew."

"Chapter twelve, verse thirty-two?"

"Yes." Cody's gaze held tight to Christ. "How it reads, makes it seem…"

"Any snide remark spoken in anger toward the Father, Me, or the Holy Spirit, constitutes eternal hell fire?"

"Exactly that." Hazel eyes stared deep into the Savior's gaze. "Just what is—"

"Do you know who that exact verse was directed to?" Christ smiled, and Cody knew nothing said there, in that shared moment in time, would be wrong. Every question in heavy, pondered speculative thought was okay to say. Nothing was off limits.

"Who was that verse directed to?"

Christ said, "The religious leaders of Israel's day. They were the ones who said I had healed a crippled man by the power of demons. In essence, they were saying I was the son of the devil, and not the chosen messiah, sent from the Father, to save mankind's fallen spiritual state."

"But that verse in Matthew reads: 'whoever' speaks a word against the Holy Spirit, it shall not be forgiven, either in this age, or the age to come."

The Savior understood completely why Cody felt that, and explained—"When someone truly commits what was written of in the Gospel of Matthew, the Father reaches down from heaven and sears that person's conscience, eternally."

"How can someone even know they've had their conscience sealed, eternally?"

"For no repentance of sin will prick their conscience to pray out for forgiveness. But what I speak of here Cody, does not pertain to you. For if it did, hell would be the place you would be screaming out to the demons, what you just asked me."

"Just how did I come to be here with you? I can't remember, other than downing this plastic cup of anti-freeze. Then waking in hell. Then you rescuing me. But everything else is a blur."

"Before you ingested the anti-freeze," Christ explained, "you silently prayed to the Father for forgiveness."

"I can't remember."

Christ explained further, that sometimes, when a person steps off to commit suicide, but does not succeed, and later regains consciousness, nothing of the act before can be remembered in great detail—just vague, fuzzed over memories that make no real sense—like a picture postcard, cut into small pieces that have been burnt black around the edges.

"I really prayed out to the Father for forgiveness?"

"Aren't you here with me, now?" The Savior smiled.

Hazel eyes scanned out across the vast green pasture. "Yes," Cody said.

"Something else still hangs over you, that is not formed in a question. What is it?"

"There is, but…"

"It's okay," Christ assured. "Confess to me."

Hot tears cascaded down.

"I'm sorry I cursed the Father, that night, before the mirror; that I cried out, that I hated Him, and wish he'd go to hell…And burn there." Hazel eyes stared at Christ. "I was so tired of being called gay, that I took all my anger out on the Father…and You. I may have even said something vile about the Holy Spirit, too." Cody collapsed into the Savior's arms. "Forgive me. Please."

"The Father does not remember your sin, that night. Far as the east is to the west. Do you know what that truly means, Cody?" He shook his head. Christ explained, "My arms, when they were stretched out, upon the cross. East to west." Hazel eyes finally noticed nail-scared hands. Christ said, "I was wounded in the house of my friends, and will carry these nail-scared hands for eternity."

"How—"

"You must now return to your body."

"Return to my body," Cody said, "but I just got here."

Christ smiled. "There is still work for you to do, on earth."

"What if I mess up? I can be real good at that."

"You will know what to do, and when to do it, Cody."

"No one would believe any of this, even if I told them."

"You will remember nothing of your time here, in heaven, other than…" Christ told Cody to take firm, mental note of the address, 3421 West Alto Avenue in Los Angeles, California, and the name, Tom Nelson, and to tell Derek Harris that that is where the man lives who kid napped his wife, Amber, and daughter, Jessica; and to also tell Heather Stockton, not to go home for a few days and call authorities.

"After you wake from your coma."

"I'm in a coma?"

Christ smiled. "You did ingest twelve ounces of anti-freeze. But will make a full recovery as if that incident had never happened. Only you *will* suffer a strong, spiritual battle, until your faith in Me is strong."

"Wait," Cody said. "May I see the Father."

Christ smiled again. "If you have seen Me, you have seen, the Father."

The Father then breathed Cody Holt back to life, back on earth.

His body lay in a hospital bed in Hobbs, New Mexico.

21

Deep blue awaited Cody Holt when his spirit hit and entered his body. No illumination that anything had even happened, other than having slipped far off into an abysmal sleep, where dreams cease to run ram shot within the subconscious realm of the mind.

Had Cody not woke with two IV's, in and out of veins, and another small tube down his nose, to keep liquid sustenance in a constant nourished drip to his weakened body—nothing would have registered wrong.

Hazel eyes finally opened, and a congested cough broke through the silence.

Cody's vision cleared, and he saw where he lay—in a hospital bed, in a hospital room, he knew not—and felt the thickness of the IV's in his veins, and the tube down his nose. He had no solid remembrance whatsoever, that could have placed him where he now lay.

His mind drew heavy blanks, and still, nothing—as if it had always been that way; and he began to wonder if that weren't true. Had it not always been that way?

Another congested cough broke the silence again.

This time, the raspy noise woke Cindy Anderson. She was the nurse on duty, and had drifted off to sleep, twenty minutes ago, in a fold out chair, and had been told earlier, by Dr. Davis, to faithfully monitor all vital signs.

Cody Holt's heartbeat was strong now.

Cindy rubbed sleepy eyes. "You're awake, and out of your coma." She hit the button on the far-left wall to signal Dr. Davis that Cody Holt was back from the Great Beyond.

"Where am I?" he whispered in a slight slur.

"Hospital," Cindy said. "You're lucky. For a few days there, we weren't sure you'd make it."

"Which hospital?"

"Lea Regional Medical Center." Cindy smiled. "You know, you remind so much of that actor, Chaz Spivey."

"I get that a lot." Cody noticed how he slurred his words, and tears swelled.

"Don't cry," Cindy said. "It's normal not to have full control of your voice when coming out of a coma."

Such consoling words did not help nor stop the tears that now fell down Cody's cheeks—pale and void of any color. Cody was alive; but didn't look it. A trip to the funeral director seemed more in order than clear, concise conversation.

"I've seen this before," Cindy said. "But you'll be fine. Really you will."

Dr. Davis had finally made his much anticipated arrival. This wasn't the first attempted suicide he had overseen. Eight years at Lea Regional Medical Center, sixteen other cases, not exactly like Cody's, but close, had come to the fortunate care of, Dr. Davis. With one distinct difference— "No one here," Dr. Davis said, "knows who you are. The couple who dropped you off, had no identifying ID on you. They simply just dropped you off, here." Dr. Davis lend in. "Do you know who you are?"

Last thing Cody needed now was to confess his Hollywood christened name—not with Cindy Anderson still sitting there. Because if Cody did mention who he really was, the shocked reaction back from Cindy, more than likely, would do no one any good.

So, Cody kept tight-lipped about his Hollywood identity. He simply just said—"Cody Holt."

"Well, Cody Holt, lucky to have pulled through, like you did." Dr. Davis was closer now. "You're not exactly yet, out of the woods, though. Dialysis will be the next step."

"For how long?"

"Depends. You really did a number on your system with the anti-freeze. Most don't ever return after something, like that. Not like you have." Dr. Davis explained about the crystallization process in blood the body goes through when more than an ounce of anti-freeze is ingested. He also added—"And from what I can tell, you downed over twelve ounces." He turned to Cindy. "Stay here and watch over him. Doubt he'll try anything suicidal again, but never know." Dr. Davis turned back to Cody. "And after a full recovery here, a stay at Hobbs Mental Health Center, is your next stop." The good doctor left the room.

Quiet desperation and uncertainty washed over Cody. All that came to mind was to get out from where he was, find Heather Stockton, and try and fix, anew, what was left of his life. If he could. Cody was up against more than just bodily recuperation because no memory of having been in heaven with Christ, surfaced.

Not so for the memory that now bombarded Cody's recollection of the sin, that night, before the mirror. This was the spiritual battle Christ had mentioned, Cody would have to endure for a time, until sound faith in Him became rooted deep.

Faith is not true faith until tested, and tested well. And Cody Holt's faith was now about to be tested. And tested well.

Another nurse, Monica Strawn, entered the room, brushed past Cindy, and wheeled a medical cart, next to Cody.

Hazel eyes watched golden liquid fill a syringe.

Monica moved to the nearest IV.

Slurred speech—"What's that?"

"Morphine," Monica said, "to keep you pain free." She plunged the syringe into the IV and eased the plastic coated tip plunger, down.

Synthetic nirvana surged.

Hazel eyes fluttered open then shut.

A narcotic storm hit Cody—like a moonlit tide that ebbs over frothy white sand in a saltwater surf before hurricane gusts rip forth.

"There," Monica said. "Not due for another round…" She glanced at the clock on the wall. "At least for four more hours." Colgate smile. "See you then." She winked at Cindy, mouthed, 'he's cute', and then left to check in on other patients—in other rooms that lined the exact same hall that housed the exact same type room Cody was bedded down in.

"Feel better?" Cindy asked.

"A little." Hazel eyes fluttered again; only this time, that narcotic storm that had hit so hard—receded back and settled calm.

Total warmth throughout was all that Cody felt.

"Still can't get over how much you look like, Chaz Spivey." Cindy smiled. "But like you said, you get that a lot."

Though the morphine had hampered his motor skills, he was still able to raise his head. When he did—the address, 3421 West Alto Avenue and name, Tom Nelson—flashed in mind; then the need to call ICM agent, Derek Harris.

"I need a phone. I need to call…" Cody's words ceased to flow. Nothing could stop his head from resting back down. Synthetic nirvana was just too much to resist, not to let the pull of morphine have its narcotic way.

While this transpired, the demon, Tuka had watched everything; Cody regaining consciousness from coma; Dr.

Davis's anticipated arrival; golden liquid filling a syringe, in IV; and now Cody not able to handle the morphine that still flooded his weakened system. Exactly how Tuka needed Cody—all drugged out and not all there.

You shouldn't have made it back. But since you have, time to have at it again and try suicide. Yes, time to try suicide again. Only this time, do it right!

Hazel eyes fluttered open.

Cody turned his head.

Catlike, slit eyes stared.

"Not again!"

Tuka fell silent, and Cindy Anderson rushed the bathroom, dampened a towel, rushed back to Cody, and gently patted down his stitch-sewn forehead.

"Sometimes people on morphine see and feel things that aren't there." Cindy kept patting down Cody's forehead. "But you're safe."

He reached up and touched three, tiny stitches. *Did a real number on myself. No telling how the rest of me looks?* He then gazed at Cindy.

"Relax," she said.

"You believe in, God?"

Odd question. Cindy still had the towel on Cody's forehead. *Then again, he is on morphine.*

Suddenly, Cody asked again—"You believe in, God?"

Ball was now in Cindy's court. She said she did, and had faith in Christ, but wanted to know why she was being asked?

"Because I'm going to hell," Cody screamed.

Yes, you are, Cody Holt. I mean, Chaz Spivey.

"I sinned the worse sin!"

Cindy couldn't tell what was said. Cody's words, because of the morphine, sounded like garbled jargon, rather than sound English. Cindy lend in closer—"Say again."

Tuka took full advantage and threw a demonic whisper—*Cody's going to hell. Wanna join him?*

Terror gripped Cindy. She couldn't move, but was still able to say, "Did you hear that voice?"

Cody didn't have a chance to answer because Dr. Davis had returned.

"Sure your name is, Cody Holt?"

He nodded yes.

"Then why is the name, Chaz Spivey signed on this driver's license?" Dr. Davis continued, "The guy with that woman who dropped you off, who's the night auditor at The Lamplight Motel, went back there, and while cleaning the room he found you in, also found this, later." Dr. Davis waved the wallet. "Now, what's going on?"

Slurred speech. "Get...me...phone...need to call...my agent." Cody's head slumped down on the pillow. Hazel eyes fluttered shut.

And the demon Tuka let out another demonic whisper—*Hell!*

22

Hebrews Chapter 6 Verse 4-6: For in the case of those who have once been enlightened and have tasted of the heavenly gift and have been made partakers of the Holy Spirit, and have tasted the good word of God and the powers of the age to come, and then have fallen away, it is impossible to renew them again to repentance, since they again crucify to themselves, the Son of God, and put him to an open shame.

Each divinely inspired word hit Curtis Paxton. Those three utmost important verses in Hebrews seemed tailored fit to how he felt and what he felt he had done: fallen away.

Hadn't he told Amber, 'I think I may have lost whatever faith I have in God.' Yes, Curtis had told Amber, 'I think I may have lost whatever faith I have in God.' Not only had he said it, but felt it. To lose something, one must first possess that which became lost. Paxton didn't know he had never been made a partaker of the Holy Spirit, and hadn't truly tasted the good word of God nor the powers of the age to come, until he confessed, Christ, there in Grace Christian Books—guided in heart-felt-prayer by, Neil. Neil would soon have more to tell Curtis Paxton about those three utmost important verses in Hebrews.

The King James Bible was shut, and Curtis snagged his cell phone and wallet that housed the card Neil had given. The card also had Neil's phone number 213-555-5421, on back.

Call roamed.

Curtis checked his watch. Time was 6:46.

Third ring—"Hello."

"Hey, this is Curtis. Curtis Paxton. The guy—"

"I remember you," Neil said. "How have you been?"

Silence.

"Still there, Curtis?"

"Yeah, sorry. Anyway, I was reading Hebrews and got to—"

"Chapter six, verses four through six, right?"

"How'd you know?"

"Soon as you said, Hebrews, I knew what verses you meant. Those verses cause everyone to have questions. But I can tell you, Curtis: those verses do not pertain to you."

"But I really felt I had lost faith in, God. I even told my wife, so."

Neil explained—"Those verses in Hebrews, penned by the apostle Paul, were written specifically to the Jews of that day, living in Israel. That's why that gospel is entitled, Hebrews." Neil continued. "Back then," he said, "the Jews had been so firmly taught to observe the Sabbath and Feast Days, to hear someone, such as Paul, say that Christ and His sacrifice upon the cross, had become now, and forever, the Passover; that Jews of that day, just couldn't accept that, and went back observing the Sabbath and Feast Days with animal sacrifices to try and continue to cover sins.

"Basically what Paul meant in Hebrews: when someone comes to Christ for salvation, then moves back to Law and places their faith there, Christ can no longer be one's High Priest for sin. Because one has moved their faith away from Christ, to something else and His once-and-for-all Holy sacrifice upon the cross. So," Neil confirmed, "you're fine Curtis. Really you are."

A sigh of relief. He was sure he had, somehow, blown it. "Still there, Curtis?"

"Yeah," he said. "Still here." Then—Amanda came into the room.

"Who you talking to?"

Curtis handed over the phone. "Here," he told her. "It's Neil, the guy I told you about, from Grace Christian Books."

"Hey, Neil. It's Amanda. Thank you for what you did for my husband."

"It wasn't me," Neil confessed, "but the guidance and leading of the Holy Spirit. I just happen to be the one there when Curtis prayed, out to Christ, in faith. If it hadn't been me, it would've been someone else."

"But it was you," Amanda voiced. "Thank you, Neil. God bless you." She handed the phone back to Curtis. He watched her leave the room in tears.

"Whatever you said, really moved her, Neil."

"I just told her what the Holy Spirit has done in your life, Curtis: brought you to a saving faith in Christ Jesus."

"You helped, Neil."

"I really—"

"Just say, you're welcome', Neil."

"Okay, point made, Curtis."

"Thanks."

"One more thing, though."

"What?"

"You need to be baptized soon."

"How—"

"Soon as you can. Guess you don't have a church yet, huh?"

"Not yet."

"Well, you and Amanda," Neil said, "could start attending my church, Life in Christ. If you want?"

"You know something, I don't even know your last name, Neil."

"Pert, like the shampoo. Not the drummer."

"The drummer?"

"The guy from Rush," Neil said. "Anyway, would you and your wife, Amanda like to start attending my church?"

"Sounds good."

The land phone in the living room suddenly rang out. Amanda picked up on the second ring then ran to Curtis.

"Captain Spurgin's on the phone for you; said it was important."

"Sorry, Neil," Curtis said, "got a call from downtown. We'll talk later." He clasped the cell phone shut and went into the living room—receiver to ear. "This is, Paxton."

Spurgin gave the details and ordered Paxton to the station.

"Got to go," he told Amanda.

"Why?"

"Someone broke into this guy's house, hit him unconscious; then kidnapped his wife and daughter." Curtis held Amanda tight. "It's going to be a long night. Don't wait up."

Hot tears. "Please…please careful."

"Keep the doors locked." Curtis kissed her deep, wiped away tears and raced for the front door.

The sins of LA streets, once more, beckoned.

23

The rope bound around writs and feet was the last thing pulled off Derek Harris after Tracy saw Derek there, all bound up to a chair, by rope, and mouth, gagged tight in gray duct tape.

That's when Tracy went for the door again.

Instead of knocking this time, a firm turn was given and the door, to her surprise, eased open.

Nothing had been out of place, except Derek there, in the spacious living room—all bound to a chair, by rope, and mouth gagged tight in gray duct tape.

Tracy had, after seeing Jim Jackson that night at The Winslow Apartments, and the talk given to call off the ill-advised search for Chaz Spivey—decided to come clean with Derek Harris, drive to his house and explain the behind-the-back decision to call Jim Jackson, for services render, to hunt and track down, regardless of cost, Hollywood's hottest heartthrob and solid box office commodity, Chaz Spivey.

All that seemed minuscule in comparison now with what had just happened to Derek Harris and his family. How could cares for an overly pampered, and somewhat self-indulgent actor like, Chaz Spivey, that no one could presently find, even come close in having one's own wife and daughter kidnapped, out from under plain sight?

It couldn't. First time in a long time, Chaz Spivey and where he was, was the furthest concern for Tracy Powers.

"I'm sorry this happened," she told Derek. "Really I am."

Everything'll be fine, Derek kept hearing his precious, little Jessica say, *Everything'll be fine...Monkey*.

"No it won't, Jess!" Derek sprang up, ran from the living room, to the bathroom, and flung open the medicine cabinet.

The Zoxin stared.

Dr. O'Connor's advice: one pill, twice daily, hadn't been taken.

Until now.

A quick twist, and Derek had the cap off the bottle; then ushered a Zoxin onto his shaking hand. He noticed thin, tiny creases that ran across his palm. He then forced a dry-mouth swallow.

The Zoxin seemed permanently lodged.

Derek cocked his head back.

Hard swallow.

That did it.

The Zoxin slid down.

Derek Harris breathed.

Then rubbed his throat.

For a brief moment, the Zoxin could still be felt—as if the med was now a tiny obtrusion that needed a surgeon's gentle nudge to pry loose.

Another hard swallow, and that feeling of a tiny obtrusion within the throat, soon gave way to ease and relief. Still, that did nothing to stop the pain and hurt that swelled around Derek's heart. What would he do without Amber and Jessica in his life to be there when things like how they had now—closed in, all around?

Derek didn't want to think of it, let alone, face it. But he had to. What other choice was there? Act as if nothing had transpired and Amber and Jessica were still safe there, in the House in Bel-Air? Even if such ways in escapist thought entertained, what kind of stand-tall option was that?

The bottle to the Zoxin was re-capped and Derek rubbed sore wrists and licked his dry lips that still had this tacky taste from the duct tape. He then shut the medicine cabinet and returned to the living room.

A firm knock hit the front door.

Tracy bounced from the sofa and answered it.

Two detectives stood before the threshold. Paxton was first to speak—"We're here," he said, "for a call about a possible kidnapping?" Garrett, small report pad in hand, stood poised and ready to scrawl down any and all spoken statement that could be of use.

"Amber and Jessica," Derek finally said, "we're kidnapped, straight out of this house. And I couldn't do anything about it."

Garrett wrote down the statement and didn't question whether Derek had any remote connection with the sudden kidnapping of Amber and Jessica. Too much hurt filled Derek's eyes for Garrett to even fancy such notion.

Though new to the role of Detective, Garrett had been around long enough, as a fresh-faced rookie, and had questioned enough "possible suspects" during those first few years in uniform blues, to know when someone hid dark and murderous intent within the heart. And Derek Harris, far as Garrett saw it, did not fit the cruel, homicidal mold of loving and caring husband/father, turned sudden psychopath, upon wife and daughter.

That type of brewing monster did not, by any means, lie dormant in wait within Derek Harris. And Garrett instinctively knew it. Still—he kept pen pressed to report pad and listened intently on all being said.

Paxton continued—"Understand, me and my partner here, need to know everything that transpired before you called."

"I did," Tracy said. "I called, after finding Derek, hog-tied to that chair, over there."

Garrett walked over. "This one?" he asked Tracy.

"Yes," she said, "that exact one." Scuff marks from the rope were on the two front legs of the chair.

Paxton knelt down, inspected; then stood again.

"Put up a fight, Mr. Harris?"

"Until I got bashed over the head." He touched the still tender lump at the base of his skull. He had almost forgot that had even happened, until Paxton asked, if any fight had taken place.

"Just how did the guy get in?" Garrett asked. "It was a guy, wasn't it?"

"Yeah," Derek nodded, "with no mask on, hiding his face."

Anticipation hit Paxton. Rarely, if ever, does a kidnapper just barge in with no mask to hide identity.

Garrett stood, notepad ready. Tracy was sitting on the sofa.

"Get a good look at the guy?" Paxton asked.

Derek tried to recall what the guy looked like, but all that came to mind was a grainy image of a man—first at the door; then inside the house; then holding a knife to Jessica; then Amber running to console; then Jessica ordered to sit; then knife at Amber; then ordered to sit, too; then Derek standing to fight; then losing sound footing; then being hit from behind; then hoisted in a chair; then hog-tied with rope, once in chair; then mouth gagged with silver duct tape; then Amber and Jessica forced from the house by that grainy image of a man.

"That's all I remember." Derek finally breathed and sat by Amber. She gently patted his shoulder. She didn't know what else to do.

Paxton and Garrett didn't have a chance to respond because the phone broke silence and rang.

Derek raced to the kitchen. Tracy followed.

Garrett turned to Paxton. "This Derek Harris guy has nothing to do with what happened to his wife and daughter."

"What makes you so sure?"

Garrett explained his sure-sound hunch on behalf of Derek Harris's innocence; that there seemed such profound sadness in his shaken demeanor for him to have done away with his wife and daughter—got rid of their bodies, in a timely manner—then blame it on some unknown intruder at the door, set to kidnap, Amber and Jessica.

That wasn't enough for Paxton. He needed valid proof—not a sure-fire hunch of "presumed" innocence.

"You'll have to give me more than that to go on, partner."

Garrett didn't have to.

Derek and Tracy were back.

A look of bewilderment shot from Derek's eyes. Same with, Tracy. They both seemed beyond themselves.

Paxton asked, "What is it," Mr. Harris?"

"I just talked with a doctor, Michael Davis from Hobbs, New Mexico, and said someone named, Chaz Spivey, who claims to be my client, knows where Amber and Jessica are."

"Hold on a sec," Paxton said. "I'm beyond confused. You mean, Chaz Spivey...Movie star, Chaz Spivey?"

"Derek is Chaz's agent," Tracy said.

Paxton shook his head. "I'm still confused."

Garrett agreed. "So am I. None of this makes sense. Why is your client, Chaz Spivey; if in fact, that is who it is, is in Hobbs, New Mexico?"

"Chaz tried to kill himself." Tears filled Tracy's eyes. She didn't know what else to say. What words could convey the hurt she felt. She was back, close to the sofa.

"Still doesn't explain why Chaz Spivey, knows what happened to Amber and Jessica," Paxton said, "and where they're at. Now does it, Mr. Harris. Anything else you want to divulge?"

Derek said the address, 3421 West Alto Avenue, in Los Angeles, California, and the name, "Tom Nelson."

Garrett wrote it all down.

"You're saying," Paxton said, "that 3421 West Alto Avenue, here in Los Angeles, is where Amber and Jessica are. And this guy, Tom Nelson is the one responsible for kidnapping them there?"

"I know it sounds crazy," Derek said.

"To say the least," Garrett voiced.

Derek continued, "But that's what doctor Davis told me; that Chaz wouldn't stop going on, that something had happened to Amber and Jessica, and this guy, Tom Nelson was the one responsible. Doctor Davis said Chaz kept saying, 3421 West Alto Avenue was where Amber and Jessica were, and Tom Nelson kidnapped them there. And kept crying out my number, for Dr. Davis to call me."

Faintness hit Tracy. Her knees became weak. She could hardly stand and sought comfort again on the sofa.

Pressure from her weight bore down on the cushions, and the extra TV remote, Jessica had stowed away, before being kidnapped—clicked on the TV.

Color suddenly filled the screen, and a beautiful blonde newscaster, reporting the six O' clock news, came into stern focus. Her lips moved but no sound resonated from the TV.

Chaz Spivey's picture-perfect image filled the screen.

"Turn it up," Derek told Tracy.

She plucked the remote from between the sofa's cushions and was adjusting the TV's volume. "It really is Chaz, on the news."

Derek said, "I know." Paxton replied—"Let's hear what's said."

Which was how an unidentified source claimed, Chaz Spivey had gone missing from Los Angeles, California, and if anyone had any further information pertaining to the Hollywood star's whereabouts, authorities should be notified.

Number (213-555-0911) flashed across the screen.

Tracy clicked off the TV. "I don't want to hear anymore," she said; but her eyes showed more than just troubled concern. Something else other than that, weighed heavy upon Tracy Powers. She had no other choice. She had to come clean. "This is all my fault."

"What?" Derek turned from the TV, to Tracy.

She confessed—"After you left my office that day, I called this sleazy P.I., Jim Jackson and told him everything you told me, Derek. Then I asked Jim if he would find, Chaz. After Jim agreed, I hired him. Then changed my mind. Then went over to Jim's and told him to, call it off. I thought that was that, that Jim would just drop it, and not pursue it anymore. But he had to've. No one else knew Chaz was gone. Other than us, Derek. I know it was Jim, Derek who called the media about, Chaz. You were right, Derek…I love, Chaz. I always have. Ever since that first night, you introduced us."

Paxton cleared his throat. "Okay," he finally said. "Who was the last person you spoke with, before your wife and daughter were kidnapped, Mr. Harris?"

"Dr. O'Connor."

"Have a phone number and address to this, Dr. O'Connor," Garrett asked. "We'll need that, Mr. Harris."

Derek got Dr. O'Connor's card and gave it to Paxton.

"Hopefully this will help," he said.

"What about what I just told you?" Derek said. "That's the best lead you've got." Tears ran down flushed cheeks. "We're talking about my wife and daughter."

"I realize that," Paxton said. "But me and my partner still need to talk with this, Dr. O'Connor before—"

"Before you find my wife and daughter dead!"

Garrett tried to calm Derek. "Let's us do our jobs, Mr. Harris."

He yelled—"Then go do just that! My wife and daughter's life depend on it!"

The Zoxin suddenly kicked in, and this queasy, uneasy feeling hit Derek and put him on the sofa.

Tracy went to comfort. "They will, Derek. They will." She then escorted Paxton and Garrett to the front door.

"We'll be in touch," Paxton said.

Tracy nodded. "Please call if you find anything else out." She added, "But maybe you really should follow up on that guy and his address, Derek gave you."

"One thing at a time," Garrett said. "Miss…"

"Tracy Powers," she said.

"We'll be in touch." Paxton added, "A photo of the two kidnapped victims, would be really helpful. Is there one Mr. Harris would not mind parting with?"

Tracy was back with an 8X10, framed photo of the Harris family. She handed the framed photo to Paxton. "Hope this helps."

He took the photo. "Like I said, we'll be in touch."

"Okay." Tracy shut the front door and went back to check in on, Derek.

Paxton turned to Garrett. "You're right, Derek Harris had nothing to do with what happened to his, wife and daughter." Paxton glanced at Dr. O'Connor's card. "Time to pay the good doctor here, a visit."

"He won't be there." Garrett checked his watch. "It's almost *seven*."

"Tomorrow, then." Paxton was back eyeing, both the Harris family photo and Dr. O'Connor's card; but couldn't stop how the name, Tom Nelson, and address, 3421 West Alto Avenue, consumed all thought.

24

Dusk swelled across the horizon.

Soon, all trace of sun was gone, as if the splendor of light had been less than just vague rays of warmth that soon faded to nothing and had Cody Holt alone, on an unfamiliar road that lead to a different light that flickered orange bright within the front window of a distant, hillside house.

Each step had Cody closer to that distant, hillside house and the light that still flickered orange bright within the front window.

The wind suddenly picked up and pressed in. Cody could hardly breath, but his legs never stopped moving.

His heart pounded away in his chest like a fist, ready to pound through rib and flesh.

Cody was before the door.

The wind settled some.

The door squeaked open.

Warmth that flickered orange bright, from carefully placed logs within the fireplace, gently greeted Cody. He was drawn in.

The door slammed shut and locked.

Hazel eyes stared at the fire that now blazed in a much brighter degree. Flames from that all-consuming fire had Cody in a trancelike state—mesmerized. His stare could not be shaken nor broken from the orange bright flickers that reached out.

He turned to run but his legs were suddenly constricted tight by a large serpent that coiled its way up.

"Planning to go somewhere?" the serpent hissed.

Flames from the fireplace shot out and burned the distant, hillside house away, except for a circular piece of wood flooring that still held safe—Cody and the serpent from hell's pit below.

"Nowhere for you to run, Cody," the serpent hissed. "Except, hell. I'm you."

"No!"

"*Sad but true!*" The serpent squeezed down hard with another coiled grip, scales scrapping along tender, human flesh. The serpent dislocated its massive jaws.

Force from the serpent's jaws, on Cody's skull, caused hazel eyes to burst forth from sudden collapsing sockets.

Then something other than the serpent suddenly shook Cody; and this sense of being lifted up and out of that all-consuming fire, overwhelmed.

Another fitful shake came and shook Cody. Hazel eyes fluttered open.

Cindy Anderson stared. "You were having a bad dream," she said. "You kept screaming, no."

Exhausted lungs breathed in fresh air, and Cody was back at Lea Regional Medical Center, far from the dream, locked within that distant, hillside house of hell's flames and the serpent that coiled its way up.

"I was in hell," Cody said. He turned away; so did, Cindy. She walked back over to the fold-out chair, next to the door, and sat.

Neither could look the other in the eye. This awkward silence soon engulfed the room and seemed to mask over any and all emotion. Cindy and Cody were at odds. Not with each other, but that awkward silence. At least, that's how it felt.

Tuka lurked in the corner. The demon just sat there, biding time for the right moment upon which to spiritually attack.

The spiritual attack came.

This time Cody, you won't be so lucky. I might even have a go at her again, that nurse. What's her name? Cindy? Yeah, Cindy. That's her.

A subtle breezelike feeling came over her, and she got up and went over to Cody.

Next to his bed was another fold-out chair. Cindy sat.

"Why do you think you're going to hell? You told me that, remember?"

Cody slowly gave his reason and told of the night before the mirror and all that was said and how the sin of cursing God, fourteen-years ago (or was it fifteen?) had now come to drag him straight to hell, to burn there, in agony, for eternity.

"You don't really believe that, do you?" Cindy was taken aback. She had never heard of something like what Cody had just said.

"Read Matthew, Chapter twelve, verse thirty-two." Hazel eyes stared. "Go ahead. Get a bible and see if I'm not telling the truth." Bibles were the one thing hospitals always kept stocked, and Cody's room was no different.

There.

Bedside table.

Top drawer.

Lay—The Holy Bible.

Cindy opened the Holy inspired text, checked the glossary, and flipped to the Gospel of Matthew, Chapter 12, verse, 32.

Christ Jesus warned: and whoever shall speak a word against the Son of Man, it shall be forgiven him; but whoever shall speak against the Holy Spirit, it shall not be forgiven, either in this age, or the age to come.

The Holy text was closed and gently placed back in the drawer of the bedside table. Cindy turned to Cody. "I think you may be taking things out of context."

"Did you hear what I told you, I did. I cursed God!"

It finally dawned on Cindy: here she sat, next to Hollywood's hottest heartthrob, and wasn't fazed. All Cindy saw was a man, in primed youth, who had just returned from a failed suicide attempt, two days prior, and was terrified of slipping further off the edge of an already fractured, spiritual breakdown—with no way of knowing how to resolve it, other than by prayer.

That's when Tuka moved in, satanic whisper—*Prayer won't help now, Cody. Lucifer has your soul, deep within the confines of hell.*

Hazel eyes watered with tears. They streamed down flushed cheeks. Cody turned away.

But Tuka was still there.

Tears won't help, either. Now, just how should taking your life this time, play out? I know. I won't have you do it, Cody. But her. Oh, what's her name? Cindy. Yeah, Cindy. Her. I'll have her do it. Doesn't really matter how you go, by your hands, or someone else's, so long as your spirit drops your body.

Tuka moved next to Cindy.

Kill him. Put him out of his misery, Cindy. Doesn't that seem, what should be done? Take a long, hard look. Dear ol' Cody there; I mean, Chaz is all laid up in a hospital bed and looks a far cry from how he does on film. Cody will never again be what he was once, on screen. Go ahead, put him out of his misery. Nothing can save him now.

Though the demon had whispered a murderous scheme, Cindy wasn't about to follow through. Aside from a tender and caring heart for others, Christ was where Cindy placed her faith. But like most Christians, when a full-on demonic attack ensues, and hell-sent influence closes in—sudden fright creeps upon and the fear that God won't answer cried prayers—overwhelms. Still, such fear as that, did not stop Cindy from sending a prayer the Father's way.

Father, in the name of Your Son, Christ Jesus and through His blood, send an angel to watch over, Cody. Amen.

Nothing had changed in the room, but the atmosphere was completely different.

The demon turned from Cindy, and an angel stood vigil over Cody. Tuka said—*Like you being here, Solan, will stop anything!*

The heaven sent angel said nothing; only placed his hand upon Cody's chest. That gently touch brought his breathing back down normal again and steadied his beating pulse from the whispered lies from the demon, Tuka.

Don't know what's going on, but trust me, Solan, Cody won't make it out of this alive. His fate was sealed that night, before the mirror. Nothing can undo what's already been said.

Leave! Solan finally commanded.

Tuka backed away and vanished.

Solan was now next to Cody.

"What just happened?" he asked Cindy. "The room here doesn't feel the same, does it?"

"No, it doesn't." Cindy was at the door. "I'll be back. You just rest." She then left to call Northside Baptist's newly appointed pastor, Mitch Taylor. Northside was also Cindy's church home, every Sunday. She knew more than just simple prayer for an angel to watch over was in dire need.

The moment Cindy's shadow faded from sight, Cody flicked on the TV.

A late-night preacher, bible in hand, quickly filled the screen. He pleaded—"Sow your one-time seed of fifty-five dollars, right now. And see God, Himself, open wide, the windows of heaven and pour out a blessing, you cannot contain. That's right, I'm talking to you there, lying in bed. Get up. Get to the phone, and sow your one-time seed of faith of fifty-five dollars. Do it. And do it now."

All that ran through Cody's head was U2's, Bullet the Blue Sky, and Bono's words: I can't tell the difference between ABC News, Hill Street Blues, and a preacher on the Ol' Time Gospel Hour, stealin' money from the sick and the old.

Cody flicked off the TV. He had heard enough.

Dr. Michael Davis then entered the room. He held Cody's medical report. "I really don't understand this." The good doctor looked up from the medical report. "From what I can tell, from reading your report, you're fine, in terms of kidney and brain function." Utter confusion still gripped Dr. Davis. Nothing in Cody's medical report added up. If anything, Cody was due for three weeks of intense dialysis. "But not now," Davis added. "How do you feel, Cody?"

"Fine," he said; then asked, "So, I should be out of here soon, right?"

"From here, yes," Dr. Davis said. "But you will still have to be admitted to Hobbs Mental Health Center."

"I'm fine. Even my medical report says so."

"Maybe physically. But mentally is all-together different. You tried to kill yourself, Cody. No way am I about to release you without a proper mental evaluation, at a proper mental facility." Dr. Davis came close. "Whether you like it, or not, Hobbs Mental Health Center is the only place to send you, I know of, around here."

"Great," Cody said. "Out of death, into the nuthouse."

"It has to be done."

"When?"

"Day after tomorrow," Dr. Davis said, "more than likely."

"How long?"

"Not my place to say."

"An educated guess."

"Four to six weeks. Maybe more. Really depends on the given diagnosis."

"Anything else, Giver of Bad News?"

Dr. Davis grinned. "After I talked with your agent, Mr. Harris, I called the authorities in Los Angeles, and said where you were; at the hospital here, in Hobbs, New Mexico, under my care."

"Did you have to?"

"Concern for you Cody is all over the national news. Being a doctor, I couldn't keep your whereabouts, secret. Wouldn't be ethical."

"Guess you had to."

"My back was against the wall." Davis added, "You'll get through this."

"What day is it?"

"Wednesday," Dr. Davis said. "The day before Thanksgiving."

Already? Cody thought. *Where did all the time go?*

Exhaustion suddenly hit.

Sleep beckoned.

Hazel eyes fluttered shut.

Cody Holt was now far from the waking world.

Dr. Davis closed the medical report, turned, walked out the room, and gently shut the door.

All the while, the angel, Solan watched over.

25

The night always seemed to tear away at Curtis Paxton. Not so much the darkness; but what the darkness itself hid—slues of missing victims of unsolved crimes, out there, somewhere—in the bleak cold-silence that surrounded back alley ways and the crime-ridden streets of LA.

Amber and Jessica would not become one of many missing victims, in a slew of unsolved crimes. Not if it were up to Curtis Paxton.

The twelve-year veteran detective had seen enough human carnage over the years, that such persistent concern for those that fell into the arms of death, in violent ways, only served as a vast reminder of the harsh, evil reality that ever so awaited the innocent.

I don't know how much more I can really take. I'm at a breaking point.

That's exactly what Paxton saw—him tattered-torn and all broken-jagged, never to be put back sound again—

humpty-dumpty. Would be almost nursery-rhyme-funny if it weren't so true. Yes, if it were not so true.

A tired and weary gaze fell upon the Harris family photo. It laid next to Dr. O'Connor's card. Paxton slowly reached for the phone, on the desk, and dialed O'Connor's number; and the name, Tom Nelson, and address, 3421 West Alto Avenue, came to mind again.

Third ring—"Hello?"

"Dr. O'Connor?"

"Yes," he said. "Who is this?" "Detective Paxton. LAPD. I was wondering if I could take a brief moment of your time and ask a few questions?"

"Concerning?"

"Derek Harris. His wife and daughter were kidnapped, early this morning."

Silence.

"Dr. O'Connor?"

He was at a loss for words. Just yesterday, Derek, Amber, and Jessica had been in the office; only to be suddenly kidnapped, just as Paxton had said; and now Derek was left alone to wonder why. "Sorry," O'Connor said. "What do you want to know?"

"Why Derek Harris became your patient?" Paxton still had to make sure Derek Harris was cut-clean from any incriminating evidence; and Dr. O'Connor on the phone, was the one person who could do just that—cut-clean Derek Harris from any incriminating evidence.

"Anxiety," O'Connor informed.

"No borderline personality? Schizophrenia? Nothing like that?"

"Nothing like that," O'Connor said. "But with all that had transpired with Derek's wife and daughter, I'm not sure what condition his mind very well might be in now. He could tail-spin-off because his mind may have become suddenly damaged and bruised. I need to call him."

"Before you do," Paxton said. "By chance, do you counsel a patient by the name of, Tom Nelson?"

"Yes," O'Connor confirmed. "But why should Tom Nelson even be mentioned?"

Paxton explained how Cody Holt/Chaz Spivey was at Lea Regional Medical Center in Hobbs, New Mexico, under the urgent care of, Dr. Michael Davis because of an anti-freeze, suicide induced coma and how Cody, after regaining consciousness, told Dr. Davis to call Derek Harris and send out stern warning on Tom Nelson; the one, Cody Holt insisted, by some divine, unknown impulse, upon waking from the coma—had kidnapped Amber and Jessica, and now had them hostage-held in a house at, 3421 West Alto Avenue.

"Yes," O'Connor said. "That's Tom's address. And Derek's client, Cody or Chaz or whoever, knew all that, after waking out of a coma?"

"Ever heard of such a thing?"

"Not from a medical standpoint," O'Connor said, "but that's not to say it hasn't happened, or could happen." He then thought of Jessica and told Curtis what the precious, little first grader had said about her guardian angel, Miguel and Christ, Himself, having suddenly appeared in her room; also how Jessica was there that day with Derek and Amber, the exact same day, Tom Nelson was scheduled for an intense therapy session about the murder of his wife, Stacy and daughter, Vanessa. O'Connor added, "But Tom didn't show. In fact, Jessica said, after I walked Derek back to the front office, how Tom left, minutes ago, and something about rescheduling. But Tom never did." O'Connor breathed. "I haven't seen Tom Nelson…well… Well, in a while."

"You're saying: Tom Nelson, same Tom Nelson, Cody Holy mentioned to Dr. Davis, was there in your office, same day Amber and Jessica and Derek were?" Paxton was taken aback. All the pieces were finally framed and sliding into place.

"Yes," O'Connor said. "Same day as the Harris family was."

Tom Nelson was a carbon-fit for the crime. There was no other way around it: Cody Holt was right: Tom Nelson was the one, and only one responsible for the sudden kidnapping of Amber and Jessica.

"And Tom Nelson's wife and daughter were also murder, right?"

"Stacy and Vanessa, yes," O'Connor stated. "One year ago, sadly." O'Connor continued, "Tom has had a rather hard go, this last year. Sometimes in therapy, Tom just stares blankly at nothing. Other times, he's engaged and opens up and express further, what's really going on."

"Which is?"

"Tom Nelson does not believe his wife, Stacy and daughter, Vanessa, are gone. Tom believes they're still out there, somewhere, in Los Angeles, living a different life, under different names."

"Why?"

"Because," O'Connor continued, "Tom Nelson never saw Stacy and Vanessa in coffins. When they were murdered on the 101 freeway, by a carjacker, both Stacy and Vanessa were shot in the face, at close range; and because so, no open casket, for either, was given at their double funeral. Tom wasn't even allowed to make a positive ID because of the damage done to Stacy and Vanessa's face.

"After that, that's when Tom Nelson came to me for counseling and slowly began to express to me, what I just told you, detective: Tom firmly believes his late wife, Stacy and daughter, Vanessa, are somehow, living different lives, under different names."

"Still doesn't make sense."

What was about to be said next would finally explain— best O'Connor could—Tom Nelson's bent motives in kidnapping, Amber and Jessica away from devoted husband and caring father, Derek Harris.

"The perpetrator with the gun," O'Connor explained further, "who face-shot both Stacy and Vanessa was never apprehended. The guy's still out there."

"And?"

"Tom Nelson believes the whole crime never happened, and the one responsible, never pulled the trigger; but was having an affair with Stacy. And that she and Vanessa ran off with him, and faked the whole crime, to do so." Deep breath. "I can't help but think, when Tom saw Amber and Jessica, in my office, his mind snapped even further, and thoroughly convinced himself, Amber and Jessica really were, Stacy and Vanessa; and then when Tom saw Derek, whenever and wherever that was, Tom must've thought he was the one Stacy ran off with to start a new life with. Her and Vanessa. I shouldn't mention this, but Amber and Vanessa's lives depend on it; Tom had, almost closed-fist hit Stacy on several occasions. She warned Tom, she was going to leave and take Vanessa with her." O'Connor also noted, "And Jessica resembles Vanessa, a lot. Now so much makes sense, Detective."

Paxton agreed. "Sure does." He had to ask, "And Jessica really saw Christ in her bedroom?"

"Jessica was adamant about that," O'Connor said, "about seeing Christ in her room. Nothing could shake her from that. And I believe her."

"Good," Paxton said.

"Why?"

Paxton faithfully confessed, "I made Christ my Savior, three days ago." He then told O'Connor thanks for all the information about Tom Nelson, hung up the phone, dialed Ryan Garrett and told him, all of what O'Connor had expunged; then rushed into the bedroom, gently kissed Amanda; told her, too, all O'Connor had divulged, and explained, Amber and Jessica were top concern now, said, "I love you," and raced for the front door; but not before holstering the 38 that still lay fully loaded on the kitchen table.

The front door shut.

Amanda locked it.

Paxton stood outside, house keys in pants pocket, looked up and silently prayed—*Christ Jesus, help me with what has to be done. And done now. Amen.*

Twilight stars shimmered bright in the dark, midnight sky.

26

Why can't they see who I really am? They think I'll do them harm. Don't they know I finally rescued them from the man who had them believing he really loved him and their husband and father? I'm Stacy's husband and Vanessa's father. Always have been. Always will be. Nothing can change that. They just need more time to come around. Then they'll see who I really am. And know that I never cast aside my love for them. I kept it bound around my heart. My heart of love for them… Stacy and Vanessa.

Scattered-brain thoughts kept Tom Nelson pacing about in sweat-drenched, sure-belief that Amber and Jessica—each handcuffed to wooden bedposts, in different bedrooms in the plush Beverly Hills mansion—just needed, as Tom Nelson surly believed—more time to come around to who he was and why he did what was done, and why he kept calling them—over and over, Stacy and Vanessa.

Scattered-brain thoughts kept coming—*The guy who had my Stacy and Vanessa, holed up in that house of his, actually erased any memory they had of who they really are, Stacy and Vanessa. Not Amber and Jessica. No. Not them. Not Amber and Jessica. But Stacy and Vanessa. That's who. My wife and daughter. That's who they are. Stacy and Vanessa. My wife and daughter. Not Amber and Jessica.*

While Tom still paced in sweat-drenched, sure belief about Amber being Stacy and Jessica being Vanessa—Jessica's wrists had grown swollen-sore from the handcuffs on the wooden bedposts and where slightly bleeding from soft, tender skin in constant, vigorous rub against cold, hard steel. The handcuffs would not budge.

Pain, mixed with fear soon crept in, took firm root, and began to ever so slowly surround Jessica. Here she was, in a strange house, kidnapped by an even stranger man, and taken far from the loving arms of her, daddy.

Derek Harris was in no better shape.

After Paxton and Garrett, along with Tracy Powers, had left the house, Derek found himself, much like, Tom Nelson (but for much different reasons)—pacing about in sweat-drenched, sure-belief that Amber and Jessica would never again be seen.

The Zoxin was of little help.

That new-to-the-market drug only caused rotted stomach sickness and an uneasy, off-balanced feeling that tick-tocked Derek Harris into a disillusioned sway of overt worry that never let up, nor ceased hitting with sick-sudden grief—grief for not taking a brave stand against the strange, unmasked man who barged past the front door, knife in hand—and hustled Amber and Jessica apart; then smashed down hard upon Derek's skull with white-blinding rage—a fist-clenched, rusted—metal pipe.

Derek truly believed, Amber and Jessica would soon be found—stone, cold dead, out there, somewhere—on the streets of LA.

Neither knew the inner pain that had engulfed and enraged, Derek Harris, devoted husband and loving father, especially precious, little Jessica.

Her thoughts streamed together in a quick explosion of trying to grasp what was truly happening—*wonder how daddy's doing bet he's real worried about me and mommy something about that man downstairs isn't right like he did what he did because he's sad over something done a long time ago and it can't be fixed but thinks me and mommy are the way to fix whatever happed to Stacy and Vanessa I think that's their names but me and mommy aren't Stacy and Vanessa I just wish the man downstairs knew that and would let me and mommy go I miss my daddy I wish he were here so he could protect me and mommy from the man downstairs I don't ever want to grow up because grown-ups make things all crazy like what's going on with the man downstairs.* What Jessica didn't know was that her guardian angel, Miguel silently watched over. The angel had been divinely told though, to stand down.

From the adjoining room, opposite where Jessica still lay, handcuffed to the wooden bedposts, she heard the door open/shut and Tom Nelson, through the walls, tell Amber—"I have to keep you and her like this, until you both realize, you're really Stacy and Vanessa. I don't want it to be like this, but there's really no other way, Stacy."

"I'm not Stacy. My name is Amber Harris. And my husband is, Derek Harris, ICM agent." Amber glanced at her wrists, also slightly bleeding from having rubbed tender skin in a constant, vigorous rub against cold, hard steel. And like Jessica—the handcuffs for Amber hadn't budged. She couldn't take anymore and cried, "Just let me and my daughter go...Please. Just let us go."

"Where to?"

"Back home."

"You are home, Stacy. Can't you see that? You and, Vanessa...Are home. Here. With me...Finally."

"I'm not Stacy," Amber cried again. "And Jessica is not, Vanessa. She is not your daughter, and I am not your wife!"

"Oh, yes you are," Tom said. "You just don't remember. But you will. Yes, you will. You and, Vanessa."

"No, I won't," Amber cried. "And neither will, Jessica. Because she's not, Vanessa. And I'm not, Stacy. And never will be."

"Not with that attitude." Tom leaned in. "But in time, things will come clear, and you'll know who you really are." Whisper in ear, "Stacy Nelson...My wife."

"Just let us go."

"Back to that again, Stacy?"

"I'm not Stacy!"

"See," Tom said, "you haven't even allowed yourself to try and break free from the bond that guy—"

"Derek Harris...My husband...Not you. You've never been my husband...Can't you see that?"

Tom smiled. "Who I see is a woman who's had a long ordeal, far from home, and can't tell truth from some made-up fiction, that guy—"

"Derek Harris," Amber cried. "My husband!"

"Hush-hush." Whisper in ear, "Voices carry." Tom smiled again. "Wouldn't want Vanessa, in the other room, to think we're fighting." He was up, off the bed, away from Amber, and at the door. "I should really go and check on her. No telling what Vanessa's thinking. Probably, we're fighting. What, with how your all tore up and screaming about it."

"Stay away from her!"

"Why would I want to stay away from my own daughter? You really need to let reality sink in and get back to knowing who you were before the "supposed" accident, that took you and Vanessa away from me."

The door closed, and Amber wept hot tears.

Tom was now down the hall, singing, "You were always on my mind." He headed for the exact room, Jessica still lay in.

Then—*Hate to be the bearer of bad news, Tom, but Stacy and Vanessa will never again regain knowledge of who they really are. Nothing can be said or done to change that. They will always see themselves as, Amber and Jessica. Not Stacy and Vanessa. Even your love for them, Tom, can't shift their minds back to how it was with you, nor the memories you so desperately cling to: your marriage to, Stacy, and raising Vanessa as your beloved daughter. It's time to give up and accept that sad fact, Tom.*

Disbelief crept in, stopped him and had him silently conversing with the demon summoned from the ethos, through intense Wicca worship and deep, transcendental meditation.

That's not true. Soon, they'll know who they are. And who I am. They have to. Just have to. This can't go on much longer.

Tom briefly rested in the middle of the hallway—steps away from the door knob that, once turned, would gain entrance to the room Jessica was in.

You're right, Tom...It can't.

What should I do?

Only one thing to do, to have you back with Stacy and Vanessa.

What?

Really want to know?

Yes.

Kill them. Then take your own life. It's the only way, Tom.

I can't.

If you loved them and wanted to be with them again, you could. Without doubt, you could.

I can't.

If you want back with Stacy and Vanessa, you could, Tom. Think about it: you and Stacy and Vanessa together again... Forever. Sounds beautiful, doesn't it, Tom?

Yes.

What are you waiting for?

I don't want to hurt them.

You won't. You'll be setting them free. To be with you, once more. Forever. Never again to leave your side. As the demon kept this lie-drive rant force-fed to Tom, Jessica, moments before, had prayed for Christ Jesus to appear and alter the out-come that seemed sure-set, not to end well.

Tiny eyes closed again and Jessica prayed again.

But Tom's voice was close, outside the door, close.

"There has to be some other way. I can't kill them."

Shut up, Tom! Or she'll hear. And we can't have that. Or she'll start screaming when she sees you enter the room.

Sorry.

Now, go downstairs and get a knife.

A knife?

A knife has to be used to release both their souls. Time is no longer on your side, Tom. Get a knife!

No.

Shut your eyes.

Tom did.

You've really given me no other option. Now, keep your eyes shut.

Again, Tom did; only this time, the demon entered him. Tom Nelson was now demonically possessed.

A mile and a half away, Paxton and Garrett, and a swarm of black and white police cruisers, raced to 3421 West Alto Avenue, where Tom Nelson also raced for a knife. He had to release Amber and Jessica's souls.

Jessica was still deep in prayer when Christ suddenly appeared.

"I'm here, Jessica," the Savior said. "I'm here."

27

A swarm of black and white LAPD cruisers, along with Paxton and Garrett, in an unmarked squad car, quickly honed in and surrounded 3421 West Alto Avenue—while Tom Nelson, still very much demonically possessed, and still completely unaware of the police force outside—kept frantic search and pace, downstairs in the kitchen, for a knife—same time, Christ Jesus, in the bedroom upstairs—kept Holy vigil over, Jessica.

"I didn't know if you were ever going to get here," she said, tear-stained eyes. "Sorry I doubted."

Christ lovingly smiled. "I'll never leave you nor forsake you, Jessica."

"Put that in writing."

Christ smiled again. "It already is."

"Where?"

"In the bible." Christ stroked her thick mane of sandy blonde hair. "When you read the Holy text, you will find that which I just spoke."

Fear no longer gripped her. "I know how to read. Pretty good, too. Got an A, last report card."

Christ smiled again. "I know."

"What's it like to know everything?" Jessica's missing-front-tooth smile stretched across wide. "Wait, hold on… What am I thinking, right now?"

"How you wish you were home."

"Nope," Jessica said. "I wish I were in heaven."

Christ grinned. "Heaven is your home."

"Okay, Mister Smarty Pants, what am I thinking—"

Jessica's words were cut short from the front door, downstairs, being knocked clean off brass hinges by a steel battering ram.

Chucks of shattered oak, scattered across the floor, and Paxton and Garrett bum rushed inside and found Tom Nelson, still in the kitchen, still in a frantic pace and search for a knife that could not be found. Before Christ had appeared, He had vanquished, all life-ending and flesh-piercing utensils from the kitchen cabinet. Even Tom's shaving kit and razor, upstairs in the bathroom, vanished.

Christ closed His eyes and prayed to the Father. The prayer upon request was answered, and the Beverly Hills mansion fell stealthily silent. Nothing moved, except Jessica's slow, beating heart. "What'd you do?"

"Stopped time." Christ closed His eyes prayed again, and the handcuffs around Jessica's tiny wrist, loosened and slipped freely away and slid off the side of the bed.

Jessica rubbed sore skin. "Thank you so much."

"Here," Christ smiled. "Let me see your wrists." They were healed upon touch.

No deep mark on either wrists now would ever show lasting scars to draw cruel attention from even crueler people. Like the tiny scar above her left eye, Christ, once more had healed, Jessica.

It finally dawned on her. "Where's Miguel?" The heaven sent angel had never materialized.

"I told Miguel," Christ said, "that I would resolve this."

"Don't tell Miguel this," Jessica said, "but I'm glad it's You that's here, instead of him." Sad eyes stared at the Savior. "I know that's bad…Please don't be mad at me." A nail-scared hand stroked Jessica's thick, sandy blonde hair. "That was bad," she said. "Wasn't it?"

"No, Jessica, that wasn't bad."

"Thought I might have done the big S."

Christ knew but asked, "Big S?"

"Sin." Jessica's head sunk into the arms of the Savior.

He raised her tiny chin and wiped away tears. "You did not sin, Jessica." Christ smiled, "Besides, who better to have by your side, than me?" The Savior then asked, "Now, how about I get you out of here?"

"Please do."

Jessica took the Savior's nail-scared hand and was lifted up, off the bed, and walked slowly out of the bedroom—downstairs.

Her and the Savior passed by Paxton, Garrett, a slew of uniformed dressed police officers, guns drawn; and of course, Tom Nelson. The room of bodies were all frozen-stiff in a time-stand-still of what appeared to be, motionless stone—formed of flesh and blood.

"They look weird, like that." Missing-front-tooth smile. "Sure do," Jessica said. "They look weird."

Christ smiled. "A little, don't they?" The Savior was now at what was once the front door, about to guide Jessica out, when she noticed the one who had kidnapped her. She stopped, looked into the Savior's eyes, let go of His nailed-scared hand, and angrily rushed, Tom Nelson.

"Why did you take me and my mommy away?" Tear-stained eyes. "Why? We didn't do anything to you. Sure didn't." Hot glare. "Can't believe I was even nice to you, that day, at Dr. O'Connor's office."

Christ approached. "Jessica."

She turned from Tom Nelson and stared up at the Savior.

A solid reason from His lips pierced the air and explained why Tom Nelson did what was done. Christ explained further, how Tom Nelson's beloved family had been murdered; and now believed, because of unholy influence— Amber and Jessica were really, Stacy and Vanessa.

Jessica fully understood now, exactly why Tom Nelson had done what was done. Jessica couldn't help but whisper—

"I'm sorry what happened to your wife and daughter." Tears streamed down flushed, rosy cheeks. "I forgive you, Mr. Nelson, for taking me and my mommy away." And like that, Jessica hugged, Tom Nelson.

Tears now streamed down the Savior's cheeks, too. Flushed and slightly rosy, as well.

"Why are you crying?" Concern had overwhelmed Jessica.

A painful burden was now before Christ because Jessica—in that brief, compassionate embrace with Mr. Nelson—had finally reached the age of accountability of firm understanding, between the knowledge of good and evil; and knew the sound difference between the two; for forgiveness cannot be graciously given, until such understanding is fully comprehended.

How could Christ even explain such reasoning, without fear, once again, taking firm root within Jessica's heart, from worry of never again seeing the Savior who appeared, not once, but twice, and had rescued her from unseen harm that lingered high, in spiritual places? How? Even the Savior had to take a moment's pause and consider such explanation would be best said to Jessica, once outside and safe from what still had to be resolved within the plush, Beverly Hills mansion, at 3421 West Alto Avenue.

The Savior hoisted Jessica up, on His hip, and walked her outside. Before being placed upon high ground, she said—"That's how my daddy carries me to bed."

"I know." Christ held Jessica in a deep stare. "Now, stay here, Jessica. I still need to bring your mother out." The Savior then entered the plush, Beverly Hills mansion again.

Christ passed by the kitchen, and there was, Tom Nelson; only the voice that spoke did not belonged to Tom Nelson.

The possessing demon glared at the Savior through catlike, slit eyes and finally said—"The child may be safe, outside. But the man whose body I now possess is mine, and mine alone, Son of the Most High."

Heavenly calmness guided each step Christ Jesus, the Savior, took toward the demonically possessed, Tom Nelson. He was still frozen in a time-stand-still; and still there, in the kitchen. Only thing that did move were those two catlike, slit eyes from the demon.

Christ demanded, "Come out, Razik!"

A rotted odor wafted through the air and seemed to seep into the floors and walls.

Demonic laughter.

"Thanks," Razik sneered. "Was all but tired of being in ol' Tom there. Think more fun could be had with Amber, upstairs.

Christ stepped forth. "You are forever banished from ever entering again, this home, or Tom Nelson." The Savior then spoke Holy power over Tom's heart.

It now pulsed alive.

Deep golden hues filled the kitchen and every room in the plush, Beverly Hills mansion, was hit by divine light, sent down by the Father.

Christ had sealed Tom Nelson with the Holy Spirit. The demon, Razik could no more search out—seven worse demonic forces and return back—to possess again, Tom Nelson and make his last mental state, worse than the first.

If a person, demonically possessed, or even oppressed, is prayed over and blessed upon the head with virgin olive oil, and whatever evil spirit is then cast out; but the person prayed over is not touched by, Christ—such rebuked demon, goes forth—out upon the earth and searches wet and dry places for seven more evil spirits than the one initially cast out and will return and bring forth unspeakable havoc upon the person prayed over—until madness and later—spiritual suicide is sealed tight within a seared conscious.

Not so for Tom Nelson.

He was finally free from the tormenting impulse and desire to believe his beloved wife, Stacy and daughter, Vanessa were still very much alive—out there, somewhere—on the streets of LA, living different lives, under different names. Nor would Tom Nelson ever more indulge desire to delve deep and practice, the black art of Wicca worship, and open wide, his mind to transcendental meditation—so as to summon, through demon spirits, unknown—ancient, forbidden knowledge from the vast ether of the Great Beyond which forms the darkened backdrop and holds in constant perfected constellation—twilight stars, divinely placed—in heavenly orbit. Though spiritually free, and the demon Razik, exercised from the house, Tom Nelson still remained frozen in place, as well as everyone else, inside and around the plush, Beverly Hills mansion at, 3421 West Alto Avenue. Even, Amber.

Christ was by her side.

The Savior healed sore and swollen wrists; then touched cold, hard steel.

The handcuffs slipped off and slid away.

Christ lovingly lifted Amber from the bed, carried her exhausted body downstairs, out the mansion, and laid her, before Jessica.

"Is my mommy okay?"

"Yes, Jessica," Christ said. "She is."

"Thank you, Jesus." Jessica hugged the Savior; then asked, "Now what?"

"I have to go."

Tear-filled eyes. "But you just got here."

"Still, I have to go."

Jessica pleaded, "But why?"

Christ could no longer avoid what had to be said. "Because you have reached the age of accountability, Jessica."

"I don't understand," she said, "what does that have to do with you leaving?"

Christ lovingly explained, "Before you reached the age of accountability, you had the innocent eyes of a child who knew not, the difference between, good and evil. But when you saw Mr. Nelson in the kitchen, you fully understood what he had done was bad. And not good. And you could have only come to that sound resolution, had you not grasped, the full understanding, between good and evil." The Savior knelt down. "I know what was just spoken, is hard for you to understand, Jessica, but in time you will begin to."

Tear-stained eyes locked deep into the Savior's gaze. "Well," Jessica said. "What about, Miguel? Can't he still come and visit me?"

Sadly, Christ said, "I'm sorry, Jessica."

She wept, "Then take me with You when You go."

"I can't," Christ said, "no matter how much I want to."

Vague understanding slowly began to permeate Jessica's mind, and subtle, gentle inner peace, washed over. She now understood, best she could, what Christ had explained. Tears no longer fell.

"Well," she said, "since I won't see you again, like this, think, somehow, you could tell Miguel to show up so I could tell him I love him and say goodbye?" Tears were on the rise again. Jessica wiped her flushed and rosy cheeks.

Christ smiled, closed His eyes, and prayed the angel, Miguel before, Jessica.

"'Bout time you showed up." Missing-front-tooth smile. Inner strength then pulsed steadily through Jessica's heart. "I love you, Miguel, but guess this is goodbye, huh?"

"Only how you see Us now, Jessica." The Savior came close. "But not spiritually. Within that heavenly realm, I will be closer to you now than how *I am* now."

There was one pending question that Jessica so desperately wanted an answer to. "Before You leave, Jesus… Why is the sky blue?"

"In Hebrew," Christ said, "the color blue represents grace." The Savior gently knelt down, eye level. "So, when you look at the sky, Jessica, you are actually seeing the Father's grace, spread out upon the world."

"Well," she said, "why'd the chicken cross the road?"

Christ smiled. "So as not to be turned into soup." Miguel smiled, too.

"I'll remember that." Jessica whispered, "Speaking of soup, since heaven is so far away, You and Miguel could stay over at my house, for dinner. Could kinda be like our last supper together."

"Not today, Jessica." The Savior told Miguel, "We must go."

The angel nodded; then turned to Jessica. "But remember, Christ and I, will always be close to you."

That finally word said, Christ stepped forth and stretched out His nail-scared hands. In one fell swoop, all was normal again. Everything moved how it once did, before the Savior halted time and space.

Jessica turned; but Christ and Miguel were no longer there, at least not where Jessica could see. She whispered, "I'll never forget the time spent with you, Jesus. You and Miguel." Jessica then knelt down, beside her mommy.

Amber's breathing was normal again, and no signs of the damage done by the handcuffs, showed on her tender wrists. She finally glanced around and noticed she now lay outside. She lovingly looked up at, Jessica.

"Mommy," she said, "you're awake."

Exhausted eyes blinked. "What happened?" Chills suddenly overtook Amber. "I'm cold."

"But alive," Jessica said. "And here with me, Mommy."

Chaos soon erupted upon the front lawn and inside the plush, Beverly Hills mansion. LAPD's finest were at a loss as to what actually happened. One minute: rushing downtown to 3421 West Alto Avenue, to rescue two female victims, Amber and Jessica Harris, supposedly kidnapped by, Tom Nelson; and now LA's finest were on the front lawn, without so much a scratch.

Nearest officer, Zack Tibbet, came close. "No way where you both out here, just a minute ago." He holstered the loaded .38. "No way." Confusion swarmed around him. "What happened, that's what I want to know." He knelt down beside, Jessica. "What happened?"

"Jesus saved us." Missing-front-tooth smile. ""Me and my mommy."

"Jesus?" Confusion swarmed even more around, Tibbet. "Or some guy named, Jesus?"

Missing-front-tooth smile. "I don't know any guy named, Hey-Suess. But I do know, Jesus."

"Christ?"

"Bingo, give the man a prize," Jessica said; then whispered, "Cracker Jack Academy;" then hugged her mother. "Jesus saved me and my mommy from whatever that man inside was going to do."

Unbelief spread across Tibbet's face. "I see," he said. "Well, there's plenty of time to get facts straight, downtown." He noticed Paxton and Garrett emerging from the plush, Beverly Hills mansion—Tom Nelson in custody. He *was* the one now in handcuffs.

Tibbet rushed up. "I'll take him from here, Detective."

Paxton handed Tom Nelson over and watched who had kidnapped Amber and Jessica, be placed in the back of a waiting squad car. *At least it's not a hearse*, Paxton thought; then turned to, Garrett. "God had His hand all over this."

Suddenly, Jessica stood behind. Amber was already off to the side, wrapped tight in a blanket and being comforted by Garrett and another police officer, Jack Davenport.

Jessica yanked on Paxton's pant leg. He looked down. A heavy lump rose in his throat; but was still able to say, "Yes?"

Missing-front-tooth smile. "Don't mean to make you feel bad, but you really didn't need to show up."

Nerves settled, and Paxton was able to gather calm, cool composure. "Really?"

"Sure enough," Jessica said. "Jesus fixed everything. Got me and my mommy, over there, outta that big house, behind you. Hey, why'd the chicken "cross" the road?"

Paxton laughed and played along. "I don't know. Why'd the chicken cross the road?"

"So as not to be turned into soup," Jessica smiled. "Jesus told me that one."

Paxton knelt down. "Bet you're ready to get home?"

"Sure am." Jessica hugged Paxton and pulled him close. "Even though you didn't need to be here...I'm glad you are." She gently kissed the detective on the cheek. "Take me and my mommy home."

"Okay, Jessica."

"How you know my name?"

"I met your dad, a few days ago." Paxton choked back tears. "He loves you very much, Jessica."

"And my mommy?"

"Your mommy, too."

"I knew that." Missing-front-tooth smile. "I was just teasing."

Amber was the one who now stood behind; her, and Garrett. He said—"Let's get these two home, Paxton."

"Yeah," he said. "Let's."

A hazy, smog-filled sunrise slowly rose up, over and out upon the horizon in Los Angeles and ushered in, Thanksgiving Day. The sunrise also lit the way for Paxton and Garrett to guide Amber and Jessica to the unmarked squad car that would soon have them back home again.

From the backseat, Jessica piped up—"I know why the sky is blue...Sure do."

28

Deep slumber no longer held Cody Holt far under. His consciousness was wide awake now yet foggy from the slow-creeping cocktail in medication that still steadily coursed his drained and sluggish system. Twenty-four hours strong, Cody had been like this—alone and secluded, behind four, white padded walls, and harnessed tight within the confining restraint of a brown, cracked and faded leather straight jacket. Upon arrival, fear of hell and going there, never ceased from his trembling lips—until heavily medicated and subdued, as he was now—behind four, white padded walls, at Hobbs Mental Health Center. Cody had been delivered there, Thanksgiving day, in a fit of defiant kicks and screams.

An eye peeked through the peep hole, and the metal door to the room with four, white padded walls, slowly opened.

Hector Valdes had been assigned to keep watch over Cody. The time had come for yet another round of cocktail in medication.

"All right." Hector came close. "Time to keep you calm again." He held two pills in a paper cup; the front pocket of his beige smock also held a grape juice box. "Don't give me any more trouble." Hector leaned in. "Not like last time." He rubbed a sore jaw Cody had smacked while screaming out about hell and going there and trying not to be wrestled to the ground and harnessed tight within that brown, cracked and faded leather straight jacket.

The pills in paper cup went passed Cody's pale lips and down his parched throat; then a healthy swig from the grape juice box. Hector put it back in the front pocket of his beige smock. "Good," he said. "Now sit tight. Believe it or not, you got a visitor." He was at the metal door. "I'll be back with him, in a minute." Insulting whisper, "Fruit cake."

Cody was alone again. Wretched thoughts of hell and going there, still kept ram-shot pace in his weary mind, like an over-heated engine, on a low-oil run in the last mile-stretch before steel and gears blew apart.

Hazel eyes took painful note of the brown, cracked and faded leather straight jacket and four, white padded walls. Cody knew he wasn't about to leave anytime soon. Even if he could, just where exactly would he go? Sightsee, Hobbs? Watch fast-pace traffic speed by with brittle tumble weeds stuck to front-end bumpers? Wolf down a prime-cut steak dinner at Cattle Baron? Buy new clothes; new house; new car; then call agent, Derek Harris and tell him that his top A-list Hollywood client has decided to call it quits and has taken up residence in a sleepy, little New Mexico town, fifteen-miles from the Texas border? Or finally take Heather Stockton's hand in tender marriage?

A daydream-fantasy finally over-rode any fear of hell.

Cody Holt and Heather Stockton were now together, on a late summer day, pristine blue sky above, doves overhead in mid-flight, as a soft pour gently pelted the earth in clean drops of fresh rain.

On bent knee, ring in hand, Cody lovingly gazed up into Heather's eyes.

'Will you—'The daydream-fantasy stopped.

The metal door opened again.

Well-polished dress shoes and neatly pressed slacks now stood before Cody. Mitch Taylor had finally arrived on the scene—bible in hand.

Northside Baptist's newly appointed pastor couldn't believe what lay harnessed tight within the confining restraint of that brown, cracked and faded leather straight jacket, and held prisoner behind those four, white padded walls at Hobbs Mental Health Center.

Last time Mitch Taylor had seen Cody Holt was well over fourteen-years ago (or was it fifteen?)—few months before Derek Harris stepped in as agent and signed the high school senior to his vast, growing rooster of ICM "pretty boy" talent that soon catapulted Cody far past any vague recollection of fame he could have ever dreamt to achieve on his own; not without Derek Harris, as ICM agent, and cunning, swift-name-change, courtesy of Tracy Powers and her seductive-temptress influence, from Cody Holt, to brazen silver-screen-daydream-fantasy, Chaz Spivey.

"Well," Hector said, "there he is." He turned from Mitch Taylor to take care of other patients—paper-cup-medicated rounds.

Mitch finally said, "Is that really you, Cody?"

Clouded Hazel eyes peered up and stared. "Who are you?" Cody hadn't a clue. "Do I know you?"

"A long time ago," Mitch said, "you did, Cody."

"How you know me?"

"I was your youth—"

"Pastor Taylor!" Hazel eyes now recognized the man in the room. Tears swelled. "Leave," Cody slurred. "I don't you to see me, like this."

"Cod—"

"Please leave, Pastor Taylor."

He eased closer into the small padded, white-walled room, slowly knelt down, and sat, bible now at Cody's feet.

An icy chill suddenly swept by.

This should be fun. Real fun. That demonic whisper then pierced Mitch Taylor's ear.

My name is Legion, for we are many!

The demon Tuka wasn't alone; the angel Solan also occupied that small, padded, white-walled room. The heaven sent angel had been there the whole time and hadn't left Cody's side—set to stronghold it out with, Tuka.

Catlike, slit eyes stared.

The demon sensed Solan's divine nature and backed away, to the far-left corner; but still kept catlike, slit eyes honed feverishly upon Cody Holt and Mitch Taylor. Both were still shaken by what was whispered, above an eerie hush.

"You had to've heard that." Hazel eyes turned away. "That voice."

Solan placed hands on Cody and Mitch, and holy peace came sudden and quick and calmed their shock-filled bodies; but the demon remained in the far-left corner of the room. Tuka craved to bring forth spiritual death, more so now to Mitch Taylor than Cody Holt.

Sure, Cody had been assigned by Lucifer, to the demon, Tuka; but having a true man of God in the very same room, proved almost too much to resist. Tuka wanted them both in hell.

I have to find a way to do, just that. If you weren't here, Solan, things wouldn't be so hard to do, what needs done.

The heaven sent angel remained silent; but still hadn't moved hands away from Mitch and Cody. Determination to keep them both safe from wicked sway, kept Solan on high alert.

We'll see!

"That voice," Cody said. "Did you hear it?"

"Yes," Mitch said, "I heard it." "How'd you find me, Pastor Taylor?" Cody had been itching to ask that very question.

"Tracy Powers called and told me, you were scared of going—"

"To hell," Cody cried. "That's where I'm going…Hell!"

No doubt, you are, Cody Holt.

Holy peace surrounded the room, and Solan kept Tuka at bay even more so because the demon had slowly risen from the far-left corner of the room—set-ready to spiritually attack again. Though Solan was able to keep Tuka from any sure physical assault, the heaven sent angel could not stop demonic whispers.

Another one broke silence again—*That's right, Cody Holt, I'm back, to drag you, straight to hell!*

"Get me outta here, Pastor Taylor." Sturdy-straight-jacket struggle. "You hear me, get me outta here!"

Cody needed more than just a quick escape from that brown, cracked and faded leather straight jacket, and from the four, white padded walls. He needed Holy anointed deliverance. And fast.

"Why do you feel you're going to hell?" Mitch already knew but needed to hear the reason from Cody himself—from his own lips. It would do Mitch Taylor no good to bring spiritual deliverance from heavy demonic oppression, if the source of fear wasn't first openly confessed, by Cody.

"I know what I said. And what I said, blasphemed, the Holy Spirit."

"How do you know you did that, Cody?" Mitch had the Holy Bible—just in reach.

Hazel eyes wept. "Because I cursed God, that's how."

Solan still had hands over Mitch and Cody. The angel had been ordered to fatefully watch over, not fully intervene—regardless how bad. Tuka still waited.

"That's not blaspheming, the Holy Spirit," Mitch said.

"How I said it, sure was." Cody shifted weight, face now on the floor. "I told God where He could go." Hazel eyes were still wet with tears. "If that's not, blaspheming, the Holy Spirit, I don't know what is."

"No different than what Peter cried out, and meant."

Hazel eyes were now dry of tears and looked up. "The apostle?"

"The very one."

"What'd he say?"

"If I know Him, let me be accursed by, God."

"When did Peter say that?" Cody sat up.

Mitch explained that when Christ, by night, was brought forth before the High Priests of Israel—Peter, at the same time, was courtyard approached by a young girl who recognized that the apostle had spent time with the Savior, and said, 'I saw you with Him', and how Peter screamed back, 'I never knew Him. If I knew Him, let me be accursed by God'—denying the very Savior then, that fateful night, thrice—whom Peter had walked with for three miracle-filled years, in and around, the seaside coast of Jordan.

"After Peter spat those very words, for the third time, that's when the cock crowed," Mitch explained, "just how Christ prophesized earlier that night, would happen, before the last supper." Mitch reached over, lifted Cody up and leaned him against the white, padded wall. "So," Mitch added, "if God can grant forgiveness to the apostle Peter, for what he said, and meant, in that heated moment of irate frustration, don't you think, Cody, God could, and does, want to do the same for you?"

"I feel more like Judas, than Peter."

"Know the difference between, Judas and Peter?"

"One named, Judas; the other, Peter." Not the most appropriate time to joke; but fear of still having blasphemed, the Holy Spirit, wouldn't relent; and inapt humor seemed best to off-set the gravity of the situation. If only for a moment.

The moment was gone.

Mitch never smiled, nor laughed; yet knew, the heavy influence of cocktail in medication was what had caused Cody to say what he did. Not his heart.

Mitch continued—"Judas committed suicide, Cody, whereas Peter repented. Truly repented." Mitch explained further, "Judas may have went to the High Priests, in the temple, and tossed back the thirty pieces of silver and said how sorry he was about betraying innocent blood; but unlike Judas, Peter did not let the guilt he felt for what he had said, cause him to take him own life, on a tree branch, with rope around his neck. Peter waited for Christ's return."

"I still don't understand."

"Peter put his faith in Christ and His return from the cross," Mitch said. "But Judas held on to his guilt, to his own death. That's the difference, Cody."

Just how you'll do, Cody. To your own death. You're right. You are no different than, Judas. Why do you think you are where you are? Guilt. Your guilt. Guilt, you have come to love. That's why God hasn't taken it away. Nor forgiven you, because you have come to love your own guilt. That's just a repercussion of having blasphemed, the Holy Spirit. Your eternal fate is doomed, Cody Holt. Doomed in hell!

"Do something, Pastor Taylor."

That demonic whisper had rung Mitch Taylor's ear, too; but the man of God wasn't fazed. The time had come to do spiritual battle.

Mitch calmly opened the Holy Bible, to the gospel of John, Chapter 6, verse 44, and asked, "Are you drawn to cry out to Christ, right now, Cody?" Shivering nod. "Then that proves you haven't blasphemed, the Holy Spirit." Mitch began reading from John's gospel. "No one can come to Me, unless the Father who sent Me, draws him; and I will raise him up on the last day." Mitch gazed into hazel eyes. "If you had blasphemed, the Holy Spirit, Cody, there would be no conviction, whatsoever, to cry out to Christ. It's the Father's blessed Holy Spirit that is drawing you to do so."

Punishment from Lucifer would be severe, if Tuka, at last chance—lost firm hold over, Cody Holt.

The demon pressed in—*That man is lying! Do not believe a word he says! Cries to the Son of the Most High, isn't so simple, for forgiveness of sins. At least not the sin you did, Cody. Whoever shall speak a word against the Holy Spirit, it shall not be forgiven him, either in this age, or the age to come. Matthew, Chapter twelve, verse thirty-two. You read it, yourself. Why do you think you're so fear-fright-scared? Because you know the truth, Cody Holt: you blasphemed, the Holy Spirit that night, before the mirror. BELIEVE IT! YOU DID IT!*

Mitch Taylor took command. "In the name of Christ Jesus, be still!"

I know, Paul, and I know, Christ. BUT WHO ARE YOU!

"In the name of Christ Jesus, be still!" Mitch peered into hazel eyes. "Cry out to Christ, Cody. Admit you're a sinner and need Him as your Savior."

Cody did, and heavenly warmth filled his heart and eased any lingering fear of having possibly blasphemed, the Holy Spirit. It was as if pure light of intense measure, sought out and washed clean—that shameful, penitent night, before the mirror—when words from Cody Holt's drug induced tongue, had so vilely spout—fervent anger toward God.

Hazel eyes finally fluttered open from prayer. Cody Holt had been forgiven. And he felt it.

Past, present, and future sins were forever, eternally cleansed clean, in Christ Jesus's anointed blood sacrifice upon the cross of Calvary. Cody Holt now knew he was a beloved child of the Most High God. Another long-awaited prodigal son had just returned home.

Solan turned to, Tuka.

Whoever comes to the Lord, He will in no wise cast out. For it was written by the apostles of old, given in inspiration by, the Holy Spirit.

Tuka now knew that the battle for Cody Holt's soul would never more belong to Lucifer.

The metal door opened again.

"Visiting hours are over." Hector Valdez stood in the light of the hallway. It just happened to be the wrong kind of light.

Catlike, slit eyes glared. Tuka wanted to inch close; but before the demon moved, Lucifer gave the life history on one, Hector Valdez; then ordered—*Take him, instead. 'He'll' do just fine.*

Demonic whisper—*Should really keep your hands off the female patients, Hector. Especially those female patients heavily dosed-out on pills you give them from those little, paper cups.*

Terror-filled eyes. "Who said that?" No demonic whisper had rung, either, Mitch or Cody's ears. "Either of you hear that?" Hector backed away. "I heard a voice."

My voice, Hector.

Terror-filled eyes locked back onto Mitch and Cody.

Don't seek help from them. No longer can they hear me. But you can. Yes you can, Hector.

He was pinned against the wall. "Stay away!"

I know much about you, Hector Valdez. That, I do.

That demonic whisper now had Hector in an all-out sprint, down the hall—round the corner, down another hall—pass the nurse station and elevators—almost out of Hobbs Mental Health Center.

Shortness of breath finally brought Hector Valdez to a sudden halt, before Dr. Sayer and Heather Stockton. They were on their way to check in on Cody Holt.

"I wouldn't go near that guy in solitaire." Sweat trickled down flushed cheeks. "Something isn't right with him." Hector yanked off his work badge. "Here," he told Dr. Sayer. "I quit. A million bucks couldn't get me back to check in on him. He's all yours."

And you're all mine, Hector. Sure are. All mine.

"It's back." He fell to his knees. "That voice!"

Dr. Sayer knelt down. "What voice? No one's here Hector, but me and Heather."

And me, Hector. Really should keep your hands off the female patients.

"You can't hear that?"

"No, we can't." Heather turned to Dr. Sayer. "Hector should be checked in and kept under, seventy-two-hour observation."

"I'm not crazy," he cried. "I don't belong here…Not like the others. Not like them. I know what I heard. It was a voice. An ungodly voice." A shaking hand pointed down the hall. "It followed me all the way from that guy, in solitaire." He was now to his feet and back against the wall. "I'm not going back down there. I'm just not."

You might not have choice in the matter. Not how you're ranting and raving on about a voice, one else can hear, but you. Is that not crazy, Hector?

"You're not there."

Then why converse with me, hmmm?

"You're not there!" Hector's breath hit Heather's face. She turned away—"Fetch a nurse."

"A male one, please." Dr. Sayer watched Heather race off then turned back to, Hector. "Relax. You're safe. No one will hurt you."

Other than me.

"Can't you hear that? That voice? It's all around! Make it stop!"

Another demonic whisper blasted his fatigued mind; only this time, deep-seeded fear cut short, all screams—and laid Hector Valdez, flat out on the floor. His exhausted body now lay calm, next to Dr. Sayer.

He looked up. There was Heather Stockton—male nurse by her side. They both rushed up.

"What happened?" Dale Keeling gazed down upon Hector Valdez, still laid out on the floor by Dr. Sayer.

"Just get Hector in the nearest, vacant room."

By arms and feet, he was carried to room 34, and eased down upon a single bed.

Hector wasn't going anywhere.

Neither was the demon.

Tuka had followed, and now laid in wait, in the far-left corner—for Hector Valdez to wake.

And when you do, I'll be ready...Yes, I will.

The demon exhaled, and catlike, slit eyes followed Dr. Sayer, Dale Keeling, and Heather Stockton out the room.

Metal hinges eased shut and the door closed.

"What was all that about?" Dale Keeling asked.

No explanation was given, nor would be—for what had just transpired with Hector Valdez, was just as much a mystery to Dr. Sayer and Heather Stockton, as it as to Dale Keeling.

"Get back to your duties," Dr. Sayer said. "Miss Stockton and I will take care of whatever Hector needs." Before Dale turned, the good doctor added, "Not a word to anyone, what happened here, understand?" Dale nodded and left, down the hall. Dr. Sayer turned back to Heather. "Let's check in on, Cody Holt."

Once there, first thing said, after recognizing her—"Don't go home...Call the authorities."

29

Tranquil comfort from beneath thick cotton sheets and the warm glow of a Snoopy night-lite on the vanity dresser, kept precious, little Jessica, snug/safe and undisturbed in peaceful sleep.

Same with Derek and Amber.

All three were together in bed, in Jessica room, not about to be apart again. At least not at night. Not with the kidnapping incident still so fresh in mind.

Hours between late evening moonlight and early morning sunrise, seemed most difficult to endure. Especially for Amber and Jessica. Sometimes Derek, too. But it was with Amber and Jessica, that quick, sharp recalls of having been seized by Tom Nelson—broke passed sure-sound truth, that the forty-eight hour horror show within the plush, Beverly Hills mansion, at 3421 West Alto Avenue—was all but over and done with.

Sudden memories—sometimes during the day; sometimes midmorning—would flash quick, rise up, snatch hold, and have either Amber or Jessica in frantic search for Derek—for firm assurance, Tom Nelson would never more be there, knife in hand—to seek delusional penance from the fervent lunacy of demonic influence that swayed in such convincing ways—Amber and Jessica were really, Stacy and Vanessa—and only needed strong faith to bring them back from any deluded sense of false reality.

Gentle pelts of soft rain came in swift cascades against the window, above Jessica's bed and woke Derek. Not in shock, but in subtle reverence that life was fragile and always well worth saving. Derek no longer needed reminding of that. Not with Amber and Jessica safe, next to him.

Those swift cascades of soft rain picked up pace and also woke Jessica. "Hey, monkey." Missing-front-tooth smile. "Whatcha doing?" Wide yawn.

A stiff lump rose in Derek's throat. "Looking at you." Sweet grin. "Sorry the rain woke you, sweetie."

"Why?"

"How you were sleeping?"

"How was I sleeping?"

"Peaceful."

In that tender waking moment of shared words between father and daughter, reserved concern if any prominent place in Hollywood still remained, no longer tore at Derek with ravenous fear, whether he had lost good standing at

ICM. He cared less if he ever signed another actor under contract, for services rendered, to garnish ten percent, off the top.

Hollywood, and what it truly offered: political backstabbing; underhanded deals that cut clean, moral fortitude; deceptive handshakes, amidst late lunches with lip balm kisses to the cheek at the Ritz Carlton fund raisers that give rich shareholders another tax loophole, to later obtain, that which was first donated at auction, all in the charitable name of charity—seemed nothing less now than spoiled rants among petty adults whose self-absorbed pains never really scaled passed, pampered privilege.

That's how Derek now saw Hollywood business—shifty wants via manipulative desire to obtain wealth in power and crush all competition that got in the way of the end result: golden televised acceptance, come Oscar time.

Truth in case, Derek always saw Hollywood business and its consumed lust for top-dollar net, as manipulative desire to obtain wealth; only now, it seemed, less easy to ignore. Nor brush aside. Like before.

Since the kidnapping incident, beset thoughts in high consideration, not only to leave Hollywood, but the state of California, itself—hadn't left Derek's mind.

"Whatcha thinking?" Missing-front-tooth smile.

Derek gave a sheepish grin back. "Nothing."

"Are, too."

"D-two."

"Very funny." Jessica got the Star Wars pun.

"I thought it was."

"Really," she said. "Whatcha thinking?"

"That it's too late for either of us to be up, sweetie."

"But I like the rain, and how it sounds, against the window."

"And I like the sound of your peaceful sleeping."

Missing-front-tooth smile. "And I like being here, talking with you, and listening to the rain." Jessica scooted closer and nestled under Derek's arm. "Wouldn't want to be anywhere else…Except maybe heaven."

Thunder suddenly boomed and shook the window pane.

Amber woke, shot up and looked around. She realized she was still there, in bed, next to Jessica and Derek—not hostage-held/knife-threatened by Tom Nelson.

Derek reached over to comfort. "You okay?"

"Yeah, Mommy…You okay?"

"Sure." What Amber really wanted to say was how another nightmare had crept in and had her back there, in the plush, Beverly Hills mansion at, 3421 West Alto Avenue—handcuffed to the wooden bedposts, while Tom Nelson rested beside in calm declaration—all was well and not the least bit, wrong; just a little more time in restraints to fully appreciate the steps that were taken to pull off what had to be done and get Amber and Jessica away from the one who erased any and all memory of who they truly were.

Thunder boomed again, as if to snap Amber away from sinking back into the nightmarish realm of Tom Nelson and the handcuffs on the wooden bedposts.

"Your safe," Derek said, "here, with us."

"Yeah, Mommy…You're safe…Here with us now."

"Where I always want to be." Tear-stained eyes locked hard onto, Derek and Jessica.

"Well," she said, "I'm not going anywhere, 'cept maybe college…One day."

It was the perfect time to shift subjects. Anything to get Amber's mind off the nightmare, Derek knew, had come, once again, to take root.

"And what would you study at college, sweetie?"

"Underwater basket weaving."

That jiggled Amber funny. "Why underwater basket weaving?"

"So," Jessica said, "I could get a job at Sea World and entertain dolphins."

Derek intersected. "What about, Shammo? Wouldn't he need entertaining, too?"

"Naw," Jessica said, "just a whole bunch of fish."

"Oh," Amber said, "I see." She glanced at Derek. "I love you."

"I love you, too."

"What about me?" Missing-front-tooth smile.

Derek poked Jessica's ribs until giggles in high laughter, erupted. "And what about you, uh?"

"I don't know about me," Jessica said, "but if you don't stop tickling me, the bed's gonna be wet."

Derek kissed her forehead. "Sounds dangerous."

"Not as bad as your breath, monkey."

Derek grinned. "I know you." He hugged her.

"And you know I was just kidding about your breath." Crinkled nose. "Maybe."

Amber laughed, "Jess!"

"What?" Missing-front-tooth smile. "I only speak the truth."

"So, do I," Derek lovingly said. "Back to sleep for you, sweetie."

Amber rubbed her back. "Before you turn into a—"

"Monkey." Jessica kissed Derek's cheek. "Just like you." She asked, "What about, Chaz Spivey?"

"What about, Chaz Spivey?"

"We should go see him." Jessica was serious. "He'd like that." She turned to Derek. "After all, you are his agent, Daddy."

"Yes," he said, "I am."

"And," Amber said, "you'd like to go see, Chaz?"

"I think he'd like that…Don't you?"

"I think he would, Jess," Derek agreed.

"Good," Jessica said. "When do we leave?" Missing-front-tooth smile. "Besides, that's what Jesus would do."

30

'Don't go home, Heather. Please. I really feel something bad could happen, if you do.' This was in constant play within her thoughts. That, and the certainty of the situation Cody believed, laid in secret wait, once Heather passed the front door and inside her house. What almost made her take his advice was that sweaty-tooth worry that clung to his every word and choked out any other chance, he was dead-wrong and on some wild, paranoid flight of fancy.

Heather ignored the whole madcap con, as she saw it, because of the disheveled state that purged hazel eyes and had Cody in a quick-burst ramble, how certain he was about what had convicted him with utmost concern for the girl in high school he had a late-teen crush on, and had come to Hobbs, New Mexico, to tell so. It didn't help matters that Mitch Taylor was also there; and once clear of the padded, white-walled room—told how Cody had just been delivered from heavy demonic oppression of fear of having possibly blasphemed, the Holy Spirit, and should be carefully watched, for any other signs of mental distress.

Like Heather going home, without having first, called the proper authorities. Which she didn't. Why would she? Advice taken by some guy not seen, since high school—harnessed tight with the confining restraint of a brown, cracked and faded leather straight jacket—would make anyone, the least bit suspicious, to follow the heeded warning of such unseen danger.

Just sounds crazy, she thought. *I've never feared anyone would do anything to me, inside my house. Besides, I can take care of myself. I'm not two, anymore.*

What Heather didn't know, four miles from home, was that Xavier Torrez was already perched in the attic (an unlatched window, on the north side of the house had been his quick port of entry)—and was waiting patiently for the front door to ease open, so as to have his frantic and sordid way with Heather Stockton, and would not leave—until such depravity was done to her, leaving her bruised-battered-beat and carelessly tossed unconscious to the floor, as subtle reminder—nothing was forgotten, what happened that night—deep within the Hollywood hills, at the mansion, Heather so willingly agreed to enter and perform carnal deeds, on her first and last seedy adult film set.

That, and the restraining order she filed against Xavier, two weeks later.

Revenge had been so consuming for years, that all he wanted now—was another solid go at Heather Stockton. Only this time—fist first. *Might have to take her out. Probably should. She'll know who I am. But her mother sure didn't. Can't believe, she actually thought I was a detective!*

True.

Mrs. Stockton had been front-door-approached by Xavier Torrez, posing as, Detective Langston—in search of Heather, to question, why—at the tender age of seventeen (because of high IQ and even higher test scores, Heather had graduated a year ahead, sooner than expected)—she was videotaped doing what she did; that the fifteen-year pending child pornography case could finally be resolved and put to rest, with Heather brought back to the state of California, for intense questioning—to help bring justice against those who had so cunningly placed her there, in front of the camera, naked; then vanished, clean away, so as to do it again to other naïve, ingenuous fresh-faced virgin girls and former honor high school grads from the Valley.

She believed that, too. Almost didn't, though. Until I showed the videotape that showed Heather doing what she did. After that, her mother was in crazy tears, and finally gave in, where Heather is now. Now, I'm here, where she is. In Hobbs, New Mexico. Where she lives now. Waiting. In the attic. For her to open the front door and step inside. Get here, Heather. So, we can get this over and done with.

Xavier Torrez didn't have to wait long.

Heather Stockton was already there—key in the lock, turning and pushing open, the front door.

It closed, and the faint scent of Brute aftershave, awoken Heather's senses; then worry, "of something not quite right" hit quick. After all, only a man, and a man of cheap means, would splash on such pungent dross. And Heather hadn't had a man at her house, for well over a year. Work had kept her busy, to even worry about dating. Let alone men.

Now she had more to worry about than just dating, she feared—because the red light to the answering machine was in a flash-burst of two unheard messages.

PLAY was pushed.

Mrs. Stockton's voice echoed—Message One: This is your mother, Heather. A, detective Langston showed up here and showed me the video you did, back in college. How could you! I had to tell him where you are now. He needs to bring you back to California to question you, who got you in that situation, in the first place. He told me what you did, falls under child pornography! Child pornography. That's right, Heather. Child pornography!

Before STOP was hit—Xavier stood behind.

"Happy to see me again," he laughed. "Should be." Stalking step forward. "I'm happy to see you again." Heather inched back. "Now we can finally discuss, that restraining order, filed against me. You filed against me. You shouldn't have done that. Know what that put me through? Sure, you don't. But I do." No more time was wasted.

Xavier Torrez got busy, why he was there. Heather didn't have a chance.

The first punch hit square across her jaw.

She landed to the floor—bleeding in pain—shocked, short of breath.

Xavier moved in.

Message Two: Why didn't you just call and tell me what happened? Instead of keeping secret, like you did? Now you're past has come to haunt you. Me, too! No wonder you wanted to leave California, after you graduated. I would have too, had I done what you did! Have any idea whose seen that trash? Course you don't, Heather. Nor do you probably care. You hardly keep in touch, anymore.

Xavier ripped the answering machine from the phone and the phone from the wall—plaster chips hitting the floor.

"She just wouldn't shut up." Psychotic laughter, and a greasy hand dangled the answering machine, in a tick-tock sway that mocked. "Would she, Heather? Your dear mother. Should've seen the look on her face when I told her, then showed her, what you did, that night. Remember?"

Of course, she did. She had been there, and did, exactly what had been captured on tape; and what had been done, had been seared so deep into her conscious—like a white-hot poker to flesh—that it had taken sound biblical surety from Mitch Taylor and his own sudden confession of sins—to assure Heather, no line had been crossed that God could not wash clean and forgive.

All that didn't matter. Not now. Not with Xavier, fast approaching.

He gazed down at the damage done. Heather hadn't moved—still bleeding in pain, shocked, short of breath and still there—on the floor.

A sudden and swift kick met her kidneys.

This time, Heather moaned.

"Had to make sure you were still there." More psychotic laugher filled the house, and that greasy hand, lifted Heather's head—sweat drenched hair. Another moan. "Yep," Xavier said, "still there. Still alive. But not for long." That greasy hand reached behind into even greasier jeans, and pulled from the back pocket—a small knife—serrated, laced blade; now angled up/under Heather's chin. "Should have my way with you before I end you. But I'm not about to leave any DNA behind. Not with my record." Pressure bore down hard on that serrated, laced blade—ready to slice flesh. "This is it." So long." Vile grin. "Say goodbye, Heather." Shock overrode any and all emotion, and she passed out.

Whatever distant grace God may have held over Xavier Torrez's reprobate life—quickly lifted and faded. Nothing more could save him now. The dreaded inevitable awaited. The silver cord had just been severed.

What felt like a jagged rock to glass, hit Xavier. He too now was short of breath, on the floor. And bleeding—from both nostrils.

Crimson gore poured out in heavy streamed drips that gushed down and slathered Xavier's face—like sudden, offensive slaps of deep swelling pain that knew no mercy. Not for him. For him, it was too late. Xavier Torrez's ill-spent life on earth, had come to an abrupt end.

Every day—needle to vein heroin bump—didn't help matters along. God had made sure of that.

But worse was yet to come.

Dead eyes slowly opened and stared. Xavier was awake now, but far from alive. Death had finally arrived, to spiritually lay claim—and never more leave. Lucifer—not a demon; but Son of the Morning Star, himself, was there, to bring the severity of indulgent sin home. Lucifer wanted personal stake in the horror that would soon ensue; but remained silent-still, until…dead eyes finally honed in on the lifeless body—there on the floor. Xavier's lifeless body. There on the floor.

Silent scream—*What's going on!*

Satanic sneer—*Alasss, we finally met, you and I, Xavier Torrez. God should have lost patience with you, long before now, and handed you over. I've waited with baited breath for this day to come for much too long. Know how many times I went before heaven's throne room and begged God, forget and give up all effort on, Xavier Torrez? From the exact moment you reached the age of accountability. Why? Because I watched, with stern observation, the inner love you nourished, the first state you were born of. From Adam's loins, I do believe. You really cared less what you did, so long as what you did, got you what you so desired. Mostly, quick cash, for another quick fix. Like what you did to Tom Nelson's family. Stacy and Vanessa, I do believe their names were.*

Xavier's soul stepped over Heather Stockton—still, out cold—and huddled in the far-left corner of the room.

I don't know no, Tom Nelson. And I sure don't know no, Tracy and Vanessa.

Stacy.

I don't know them!

You should, Xavier. You face-shot them. Both. After carjacking them. Rememberrrr?

Lucifer opened the floodgates, and that torrid memory—gun in hand, pointed at Stacy's temple; then the shot fired; then the same to, little four-year-old, Vanessa—reverberated steadily through Xavier Torrez's soon-to-be-tortured soul.

Phantom tears fell.

I don't know them!

Satanic whisper—*But slayed them, just the same. I know, for I was there. So was, God. You, Xavier Torrez will have much to answer for. That, you will. Come. Time has no longer been allotted you, here on earth. You have sowed your last wicked seed.*

I don't know them!!!!!Idon't know them!!!!!I don't know them!

Neither does God know you, Xavier. So, let's go. NOW!

A cluster of deepened, hallow cries, screamed out and lit ablaze—a bright, orange glow that engulfed Xavier Torrez and dragged his eternally lost soul, straight to hell. That bright, orange glow also filled the living room with such sudden light, that the police officer at the front door, stepped back—hand in solid clench upon holstered gun.

A quick turn on the doorknob, and Luke Aston pushed past the threshold, to Heather Stockton. She was still there on the floor. Blood from her lip had dried into a small, caked trail, down her now blue and bruised chin. This would be the last time Heather, or any other girl, anywhere, would ever face the fisted wrath of Xavier Torrez.

The only thing of his that remained—bloodstained clothes and shoes. There, too—on the floor, next to where Luke Aston stood.

He knelt down and checked, fingers to neck, Heather's vitals. Sturdy-strong and full of vigorous life. Heather Stockton was very much alive, and would stay that way, until the heavenly Father called her back home.

Emerald green eyes fluttered open. Heather Stockton stared.

"What happened?" she asked.

Luke helped her to her feet and walked her over to the coffee table, by the phone that had been ripped from the wall.

Luke bent down, picked it up. "Was just about to ask you the same thing."

All Heather could recount: coming home, key in lock and turning open, the front door; heinous scent of Brute; checking answering machine; listening to message from her mother; then Xavier Torrez standing behind.

"Who?" Luke asked, report pad and pen in hand.

Emerald green eyes misted with tears. "An old boyfriend," Heather said, "I wish I had never met."

Luke looked around and saw those bloodstained clothes and shoes that had once belonged to Xavier Torrez.

"Those aren't your clothes?"

"No," Heather said. "They're, his."

"This, Xavier Torrez?"

"Yes." Emerald green eyes were now dry of tears. Heather had finally collected sound composure again.

"Then the guy's still here, in the house." Luke quickly withdrew his gun. "Don't move. I mean it."

Luke moved down the hall.

A springboard ladder that lead to the attic, Xavier Torrez had climbed up then down, was soon discovered.

Luke ascended up, flashlight in hand.

The light from the flashlight soon penetrated thick darkness.

All that was found was a barren, insulated space that made up the rather small attic. No sign of Xavier Torrez had even been there—other than two dust-laden shoe prints that were in the very far back. So far back, Luke Aston didn't notice. Of course, Luke Aston hadn't climbed the ladder to find footprints. He was in search of a man. Who, by all accounts, wasn't there. Or ever would be. Xavier Torrez and his ill-rotted soul had up and vanished, to the netherworld below—where torment and pain awaited—for eternity.

Steel-toed boots were back before Heather. She gazed up at Luke.

"No one there," he said. "Only sign he ever was here, in the house, are those clothes, of his. If, in fact, they are his clothes."

"They are," Heather said.

"Hate to ask—"

"No," Heather interrupted, "I haven't had anything to drink. Or do drugs. Recreationally, or otherwise."

"Sorry, but—"

"Had to ask," Heather interrupted again. "I know." She sank further back in the chair and gazed out the window. Nothing made sense of what had just happened. All that came to mind: the sick, deprived addiction of heroin impulse that utterly consumed Xavier Torrez, to seek out, day by day—sins of fleshly carnality, needle to vein—the next quarter gram fix—granted by violent means upon those in the wrong place at the wrong time—before the wrong junkie. Xavier Torrez, gun toting loser—forever now. And evermore.

"Stay here," Luke told Heather. "I'll be right back. And he was—clear, plastic evidence bag in hand, and knelt down and collected Xavier Torrez's bloodstained clothes, and sealed them tight, within that clear, plastic evidence bag.

Luke stood. "Don't really know how to file this one." He came close. "Other than" bloodstained clothes, found at crime scene. Other than that, I'm at a loss. A total loss."

"So am I," Heather said; then asked, "Just how did you know to show up here?"

"Mitch Taylor."

"Mitch Taylor?"

"He called with concern about you being here, by yourself, and asked if I wouldn't mind stopping by." Luke sat next to Heather. "Why was he concerned?"

"Long story," Heather said. "Anyway, how do you know, Mitch Taylor?"

"He's my pastor."

Amazement filled emerald green eyes. "You go to Northside Baptist?"

"Yeah."

"So do I." Heather smiled.

Luke leaned in. "How long?"

Question was quickly by-passed. "Why don't I recognize you?"

"Probably the uniform," Luke said, shy blush. "And gun." He stood and was at the front door, hand ready to turn knob. "You don't mind," he said, "after I drop off the evidence, here, at headquarters, and file a report, or lack thereof, if I come back and keep watch over you, outside in the patrol car?"

Heather smiled. "I'd like that."

"Good." Luke turned and gave another thorough, quick search. He was back. "House is clean. No one here...But us. Still," he said, "keep the door locked, rest of the night, okay?"

Heather nodded. "Okay."

"Well," Luke said, "problem seems solved, except—"

"Where Xavier Torrez really is?"

Luke promised, "He'll be found."

"I don't think so." Heather's gaze fell away from the clear, plastic evidence bag and bloodstained clothes, contained therein—and upon the window again; and wondered if, by chance, Xavier Torrez still didn't lurk out there, somewhere—in the bleak night that formed murky darkness?

"Like I said," Luke said, "after I'm back from the station, I'll be right outside, in the patrol car, if you need anything, okay?"

"All right," Heather smiled. "Thanks."

Luke smiled back and left.

The door shut.

Heather raced and locked it. She wasn't taking any chances. She also eased the deadbolt in place; then turned for the sofa.

She sat, clicked on the TV, and tried to let Brad Pitt—surprise, late-night guest on Jimmy Fallon, drown out any remaining fears of what had just transpired within the supposed safe place called, home.

Oddly enough, attention was never paid to what looked like the image of two cloven hooves—burnt black, deep into the oak wood floor—few feet from where Xavier Torrez's clothes had once laid.

Sleep never came.

Heather Stockton had remained wide-eyed-awake the whole night.

31

Five days from when Xavier Torrez had broke in and almost killed Heather Stockton, Cody Holt was released from Hobbs Mental Health Center. No one on staff, including Dr. Sayer, and especially Heather, could dispute the fact that the actor-in-missing had been led by more than just sheer happenstance delusion by heavy influence of cocktail in medication.

Every word of the story only solidified just how right Cody Holt had been—not certifiable crazy, as once suspected; but truly overwhelmed with utmost concern for the girl back in high school that still, somehow, managed to pull heavy, secret heartstrings.

For Cody, the passing of time hadn't hampered how he once felt; but he knew that the passing of time had certainly happened, and he was no longer in high school; and Heather Stockton was no longer the girl he once knew. For she was now a woman—in full bloom—far beyond silly, contrite teenage, hormonal impulse.

"Wish you would have told me," Heather said. "I had a crush on you, too."

"Really?"

"All the girls did, Cody."

"Guess I was too consumed with—"

"Your hair?"

"What about my hair?"

"It was your whole world, back then."

"Was not."

"Was so." Heather gently made a tousled mess of carefully streaked highlights that gave subtle shape and style to Cody's precision-cut coif. Not overly done, but enough up-keep in maintenance to exude prominence somewhere special, other than Hobbs, New Mexico, or anywhere else within a hundred mile radius. "The girls," Heather said, "use to guess how much time, each morning, you took to get each strand in place. That, and how much hairspray."

"I didn't use that much."

"Cody, you could have jogged through a tornado and come out the other side, not a hair out of place."

"Not my fault," Cody grinned. "I lay my fashion addiction to Sprtiz Forte, and at the feet of Duran Duran."

"Yeah," Heather grinned back. "Blame it on the Brits."

"Have to admit, John Taylor's hair was a planet onto itself."

"Still is."

"I read his biography, In the Pleasure Groove, last year."

"And?"

"Strange," Cody said, "John decided to open his book with him reflecting back on his mother taking him to church, when he was a child. Stranger still, how Mitch has the same last name as John."

Whether crafted on purpose, or not—the topic in conversation had now shifted to a much darker topic than just Eighties pop music—or those that composed such top-forty-friendly radio hits.

Cautious not to tread too heavy and have Cody back away, had Heather broaching the subject with utmost care. "Want to discuss what you went through?"

"Where to start?"

"Wherever you want, Cody." Heather took his hand. "Or you don't have to. It's all up to you."

"For some reason, I think I owe you this."

"You don't owe me a thing, Cody." Heather still held his hand. "I'm just glad you're alive."

"I'm glad you're alive, too." Hazel eyes stared. "Still care to hear what I have to say?"

"If you want."

Guarded words that formed a heated mental picture, flowed…

Club XTC was packed to fully capacity—four-hundred party-goers strong. Saturday night always brought out the night crawlers, like Trent Toler, pure white powder supplier, and anything in between, in abundance, for those in a mad, half-gram search for the ultimate high—like Cody Holt/ Chaz Spivey.

Straw up his nose, he had the bathroom stall latched tight.

'Take it easy with that stuff.' Trent stepped back. 'Do too much…And boom, there goes your heart."

'Know who I am?' Quick snort, and an aspirin flavored nasal drip coated a dehydrated throat. Cody suddenly coughed; then a slow, creeping rush hit his brain, crawled down his spine, back up, and dilated his pupils. Large and harsh.

'Some jerk who's probably not going to know when tomorrow comes.' Trent folded the fifty bucks paid and stuffed them in his pocket. 'I don't get you, man. Here you are, Movie Star Chaz Spivey, and can't find any other way to spend time, except in a stall, in a place like this, with someone like me.'

'I enjoy corrupt company.'

'People do drugs cuss they can't have your life and hate theirs, and you do drugs cuss your life is what they want.'

'And they hate me for it, Trent.'

'Just the guys,' he said. 'The girls differ in that matter.'

'Only at night.' Cody unlatched the stall and flung open the door. 'During the day, they can't be found.'

'Cuss you sleep till deep evening.'

'Stops the boredom from coming.'

'And when it finally comes?'

'I end up in a stall, in a place like this, with someone like you.'

'Only cuss what I have.

'Speaking of—'

I'm not selling to you, anymore. Ever.'

'What?'

'You're cut off, Chaz. At least from me.' Trent pushed Cody further out the stall. 'And I'm gonna spread word, no one else sell you, either. Stay a movie star, Chaz. Not a statistic.

'I'll be both,' he said. 'A movie star and statistic.'

'Don't work that way,' Trent said. 'Either live. Or die. You choose. Plain-put-simple. Live. Or die. What do you choose?'

'This.' Cody reached into his faded denim jacket pocket and pulled out a small, square tab of acid laced paper, not bought from Trent, and swallowed the psychedelic drug. 'There,' he smiled. 'All gone. Nothing on me to get busted with.'

'Unless you get pulled over.'

'Which I won't.'

'I know,' Trent said. 'I'm taking your keys.'

'But I don't own a piano.' Dilated pupils stared. 'Look, you're a drug dealer. Shouldn't you encourage *this strange behavior?*'

'Hand 'em over.'

'You saw me. I don't have anything on me. Just in me.'

'Car keys.' Trent came close. 'I mean it, Chaz.'

Without warning, bright colored hallucinations—in quick, flash form—bombarded what had once been an unaltered reality. 'Things look weird, now.' Cody rushed the sink, turned on the water, and splashed his flushed face.

'Cuss whatever you took,' Trent said, cell phone in hand, 'finally kicked in.' He eased Cody to the floor, called a cab, gave the location, 451 Electric Avenue, and ended the call, clasped the cell phone shut, and sat down. He knew any chance to snag Cody's car keys was beyond lost and not even worth the case, anymore. 'You're staying here. With me. Until your ride shows.'

'Then?'

'Go home and sleep off tonight.'

Which didn't happen.

Sleep no more washed over, had a tidal wave raged forth and pulled Cody Holt far under—now back home, standing in the bathroom, before the mirror.

Hazel eyes stared.

'I look tore up from the floor up. If I could get some sleep...'

Too many drugs in your system, for that. You might need to take things easy. Or you might not make it through the night.

The sudden voice that spoke wasn't one recognized; it resonated with an intent tone of sure self-destruction—aimed solely at Cody Holt.

He stayed locked in trembling fear before the mirror—unable to speak.

The sudden voice continued—*Acting not so fulfilling, anymore? Have the camera lights finally dimmed your zeal for life? Seems even your fan bas, can't satisfy, anymore.*

Hazel eyes sudden blinked.

Handsome features that once caused women, worldwide to shudder deep inside—took on odd shapes, melted, and dripped clean from Cody's face. The acid-laced paper ingested, mere hours ago, had given Lucifer all the leeway needed. Cody Holt, still locked in trembling fear before the mirror, and still unable to move—had, for years—been a sight set strong for The Son of the Morning Star.

Lucifer took full advantage.

Such a sad state of human waste. Do you know that God can't stand you? Never could. That's why I'm here, speaking to you... To finally say: your life is not something God deems worth saving. You, Cody Holt, are a lost soul.

Fear-frozen words finally broke silence—'That's not true!'

Take another gander at that face of yours. Or what's left of it.

'It's the drugs! What's happening, isn't happening!'

Dig into the sink. See if your hand doesn't come up with pieces of your melted face. Go ahead. Do it. See, if what I say, isn't so.

An uncontrollable urge suddenly took hold and would not wane. Cody couldn't help himself. He had to see, if what lay in the sink, really had once been his face.

Hazel eyes shut tight, and a shivering hand toyed around, until what felt like raw chunks of wet meat slipped through quivering fingers. No mistake, the drug-induced hallucination had now become real. All too real. Too real to be ignored.

Cody screamed—"No!"

Yessss. What's left of your once beautiful face is slipping through your fingers. Try finding a plastic surgeon to fix that. Like I said, you're not worth saving. And God hates you. All this can change, though.

'How?'

Curse God. Tell him, you hate Him.

'No.'

If God really loved you, would He let any of this happen? I think not. Might as well tell Him how you feel…How you truly feel.

'He's not doing this…You are!'

But He's allowing it. He is God. And what He wants, He allows. And what it seems He's allowing now, is me here with you, so as to let you know where you truly stand with Him. Which is not in good grace, anymore. Not at all.

'I won't curse God!'

Sure about that?

'Yes.'

Really?

'Yes, really.'

Oh, I think you will…Especially with what's still happening.

'It's the drugs!'

No. It's your face, Cody. It's still slipping through those trembling fingers of yours. Of course, you do have this in your favor: no one will ever again think you're gay. Of course, no one will ever again look at you. Give and take. That's what life is really all about, anyway: give and take. And I have a distinct feeling, Cody, you can't take much more. Not with what's still happening with your face. Go ahead, peek another gander.

Hazel eyes stared again; only now—partial skeletal remains, along cheeks and chin—shone bone-white-bright through decayed strips of molten flesh that pierced the reflective glare of the mirror—set sure now, it seemed, never to release Cody to any sound form of safe reality again. He was trapped within a hallucinogenic hell of his own making, with no way to alter—the inner pain, personified.

This was too much. He needed out. Only he didn't know how.

Lucifer bore down.

Where is God in all this, Cody? In heaven, that's where. Looking down…Laughing. At you. You, Cody Holt…Or is it, Chaz Spivey? Hard to tell, anymore, isn't it. But how you feel, isn't…Is it? Get over it, Cody. Curse, God. Tell him how you hate Him for what's He's having you go through, what He's had you go through your whole life. If He had really loved you, would He have allowed all those snide remarks about you being—

'I'm not gay!'

I know you're not. You know you're not. But no one else sure does. How many times, back in school, even now, did comments circulate about your sexuality? And how for sure, everyone knew, without doubt, you were gay? Sad, really, how nothing you did nor said, altered the thoughts people had of you. Here, want to feel all that again? Just to make sure?

Swift, inner pain, when speculation arose, whether Cody Holt was gay—hit with quickened force, and dropped him to the floor—knees now swollen and bruised from the hard impact.

Same for you now, as it was back then. Nothing's changed. People will always assume you have a thing for the other team. Even women you've bed down, can't help but think you're set to jump fence and go rogue. Why? You understand women way too well. Even for your own good. And that makes women nervous. For they have been conditioned, since childhood, through worried parents, and even from my own late night whispers, that if a boy, or man, is somewhat sensitive, he must have a strange, hidden secret, buried deep in the closet. Games I just love to play on the human race. I'm the reason for all this, you know. Oh, look at me, in one of my long rants, again. Seldom, though, do I get such one on one time with an earth bound misfit, like yourself, Cody Holt. Still in emotional pain?

'Yes.'

Then, go ahead…Pray.

'To—'

God…Yes. Pray to God. Here, I'll even help in that matter. Now, sneak back upon the mirror, Cody.

He did. His face no longer held disfigured features; once again, handsome—and ever so, camera ready.

Go ahead now...Pray.

Hands clasped tight together.

Hazel eyes shut.

Cody prayed.

Only no divine mercy fell upon his midnight cry.

Lucifer had left out one vital key: prayers do not reach the father, unless prayed in the name of His Son, Christ Jesus. For no one comes to the Father but through the name of His only begotten Son.

Satanic whisper—*Get a busy signal? Don't feel bad. You're not alone. God hates the entire human race. I'll let you in on something: no one's prayers get answered. Not a one. From anyone. That's why so much suffering bears down and grinds into all you helpless, earthbound misfits. Oh, God isn't dead; but He most certainly is to everyone here on earth. I know. I watch in spirit, babies suffer in hospitals, while tears drip in prayers from desperate parents; I watch in spirit, husbands beat wives bloody, while tears drip in prayers from desperate children; I watch in spirit, rapes, murders, and every other form of depravity, torture the weak and innocent, while tears drip in prayers from the victims. Much how your own tears, while in prayer, dripped in the same sad fashion; and did God arrive, to deliver you, Cody? Don't answer. Had He, you and I wouldn't be in conversation, would we? Now, go on...sneak another peek, there, before the mirror. See if I'm not right.*

Fear consumed hazel eyes. Cody's face, once again, had returned to a melting, dripping mess.

'Make it stop!'

Satanic whisper—*You know what to do…*

———

"So…" Cody Breathed, "I cursed God…With everything I had." Tear-filled hazel eyes. "I was so convinced God hated me…My whole life." Tears finally streamed down flushed cheeks, and hazel eyes latched onto, Heather Stockton. "I should've had more integrity, than to do what I did, that night." Cody's head slumped. "I really thought, for sure, I had blasphemed, the Holy Spirit, and that there was no eternal redemption left…Not for me."

"Mitch thought he had done the same thing, too."

"Yeah," Cody said, "he told me that."

"But he didn't," Heather said. "And neither do you, Cody."

"If you'd seen what I had, and heard what I did, before Mitch found me, in that padded room…You might've thought the same thing." Hazel eyes blinked. "I don't ever want to go there, again."

"You won't."

"My mind might take another flip-flop." Cody still needed slight assurance that Hobbs Mental Health Center and that brown, cracked and faded leather straight jacket and padded white-walled room would forever remain locked away in guarded stance from ever being used again.

"You're not crazy, Cody." Heather smiled. "Or I wouldn't be here with you."

"What about when I leave?"

"…Cody."

"Sorry," he said, "had to ask."

"It's just…too much—"

"Time has passed." Cody gave a silent wish for it not to be so; even though he knew the harsh truth.

"Sadly." Sorrow overwhelmed Heather's heart.

Hazel eyes swelled with tears again. "Why does time alter, what could have been?"

"I don't know…But it does."

Caught up in a daydream life together, had things gone different, Cody and Heather—didn't see precious, little Jessica enter the room—hair still damp.

"Whatcha doin'?" Missing-front-tooth smile. Derek and Amber were not far behind. Their hair was still damp, too.

"Jessica," Amber voiced, Derek right behind, "what did I tell you about sneaking up on people, like that?"

"That's not people…That's just Chaz Spivey." Jessica gave a silly wink. "No big deal."

"She's right," Cody said. "I'm no big deal."

Derek stepped forth. "Yes, you are, or else I wouldn't have signed you as a client."

"That was a long time ago," Cody said. "Times change… So do movies."

"What are you saying?" Derek was now holding Amber's hand.

Cody breathed. "I might give up the whole Hollywood thing."

"Seriously?" Heather asked.

Hazel eyes beamed bright. "Yes."

"But you can't," Jessica said. "Just can't."

Cody knelt beside. "Why?"

"No one else," Jessica said, "could play Jesus...But you."

"Why would I play, Jesus?"

"Because you're the only actor I would want to."

"Want to?" Cody didn't know what Jessica meant; but was soon to find out.

"Play Jesus," she said, "in my story about Him." Missing-front-tooth smile. "You're the only one I would to play Him."

"You have a story about, Jesus?" Cody smiled.

"A true one." Jessica hugged Cody, pulled him close, and whispered, "Bet you do, too."

In that tender moment shared between screen idol and sweet, precocious first grader, Heather's heart softened in warm desire for children of her own, to nurture and raise, before time ushered in, no blessed chance to conceive.

Amber sensed what Heather felt, and told Derek, "She wants children."

Soft whisper, "Really?" Derek smiled.

Soft whisper back, "Yes, really. Can't you tell?"

There was no time to reply.

Mitch Taylor had entered the room.

"Ready, Cody?"

That said, Mitch Taylor guided Cody Holt out of the room, to a small baptismal pool, insulated behind a plush, velvet curtain. There were two-hundred-plus congregation that sat silent-still in reserved reverence to the metaphorical cleansing of sin that was about take place. Derek Harris, Amber, Jessica, and Heather Stockton, were among those there seated quietly in the first pew.

Cody stood before the small, fiberglass encased stairs; then slowly entered the jet-propelled flow of warm water that rose high above his now submerged waist. This moment of public declaration, in claiming Christ Jesus, as one's personal Savior, would be forever celebrated in Holy remembrance of accounted deeds, marked down upon eternal pages within the Book of Life that proclaimed, Cody Holt was forevermore cleansed from sin by the righteous blood of the heavenly Father's only begotten Son, Christ Jesus.

Mitch took Cody's hand, stood him square-straight in the middle of the baptismal pool, and turned him due east.

"I baptize you in the name of the Father, the Son, and the blessed, Holy Spirit."

When Cody arose from the warm flow of jet-propelled water, the congregation rejoiced—"Amen!"

It wasn't seen nor sensed, but Christ was there, guiding Cody back up the stairs to the room again to dress.

What covered him now was not cotton fibers sewn in constructed pattern and shape by corruptible human hands, but instead—divine grace from above, granted in loving splendor from the heavenly Father.

Tender silence swiftly surrounded Cody.

He knelt and prayed—*Christ Jesus, I come in prayer, in Your name, and through Your blood, that You lift and protect my words to the Father. Thank you for never giving up on me, though, I gave you every reason to. Thank you for Saving me. Not only from my own corrupt blindness but when I tried to take my own life. A life You gave to me. Please understand, this is my first real time, with You, in prayer. I've been told my Mitch, all You really want, are words spoken from the heart. Which is something new. Most of my life, I've only repeated words from the page. Guess You already knew that, though. You know, I don't want to act, anymore. Just seems silly. Especially now, with all I've gone through, in the last few days. Which really, I guess, is something I've been going through, my whole life. I just didn't know it. Until just here recently. Please forgive me for being so late. Thank You for listening. But mostly, thank You for sending Your Son, Christ Jesus, in my place, upon the cross. Amen.*

Before Cody rose from bent knee, Mitch Taylor had entered the room and watched in quiet solace—the young man he once knew, all those years ago, when what mattered most, was the endless pursuit of fame and playing the Hollywood game—there now, in humble prayer, before the Lord.

Tears swelled.

First time, in a long time, Mitch Taylor actually felt his heavenly anointed calling upon his life had made a lasting difference that would transcend passed a pristine, well-cleaned and freshly vacuumed office. Sure there had been, many times before, wayward souls that had been lead to the Lord—even breaking free—the torrid chains of heavy demonic oppression of fear in having possibly blasphemed, the Holy Spirit; but nothing as profoundly intense as with, Cody Holt. This, Mitch Taylor knew. He also knew, through solid prayer—such spiritual warfare, as that— would nevermore cross his path. Mitch Taylor had fulfilled his pastoral duties, as saintly exorcist, in that area.

"Cody?"

He turned. "Yes."

"The congregation, 1 believe, would like to hear your testimony. That is, if you're up for it?"

Bombardment of tiny, racing footsteps, filled the room.

"Whatcha doin'?" Missing-front-tooth smile.

Gentle smile back. "Just talking," Cody said.

"About?"

More racing footsteps suddenly bombarded the room. "Jessica," Amber said, Derek by her side, "you're not suppose to be in here."

"That's right," Derek said. "You just ran off...Why?"

"Had to make sure Cody, there, wasn't drowned."

"Hadn't drowned," Amber corrected. "And you can see, he's still breathing, Jessica."

"You know what I mean."

Mitch smiled. "She didn't interrupt anything important. Really she didn't."

Cody agreed. "Nope," he said. "Jessica sure didn't."

"So," Mitch said, "think you're up to giving your testimony?"

"What's that?" Missing-front-tooth smile. "Testimony?"

Cody saw the wonderment that surrounded Jessica. "You'll see in a minute." Hazel eyes then locked onto, Mitch Taylor. "I'd love to give my testimony."

He led the way, followed by Derek, Amber, and precious, little Jessica. Cody Holt was last to leave the room; but was stopped in the hall by golden beams of a breathtaking sunset that cascaded through the double-wide glass door. Cody wanted a moment to take this in.

He walked outside, breathed deep—fresh fall air—and stood in silent spellbound-awe at those last, warm golden rays of setting sun which spread ominously out, across a timeless horizon that stretched forth to heaven. *Thank you again, Father for never giving up on me.*

Cody's silent moment was suddenly interrupted by a gentle poke to his ribs.

"Whatcha doin' out here?" Missing-front-tooth smile.

Hazel eyes glanced down. "That's not the real question," Cody said.

"Then, what is?"

"What *are you* doing out here?"

"Just keepin' tabs on you."

"Oh, I see."

"Scared, aren't you?"

"About?"

"Your testimony…Whatever that is."

"Kind of."

"Don't worry…" Missing-front-tooth smile. "…I'll *save a prayer* for you."

Cody stared deep, one last time, into the warm, golden rays of the fading *sunset*, briefly sighed, and turned back to Jessica. "Best we get on inside, now."

"After you dear, Sir."

"Why not together?" Cody lifted Jessica up and placed her on his hip.

"You know," she said, "this is how my daddy carries me to bed." She added, "Why'd the chicken cross the road?"

"I don't know."

"So as not to be turned into soup." Missing-front-tooth smile. "Jesus told me that one. I also know why the sky is blue…Sure do." Precious, little Jessica then rested her head gently upon Cody Holt's shoulder.

He felt her tiny, rhythmic breathing in perfect time against his chest, sighed again, and carried Jessica back into church—unaware, that from high above—the Father, Christ Jesus, the blessed Holy Spirit, and the angels, Miguel and Solan—smiled and watched over.

Life was new.

Epilogue

*F*ew weeks upon returning to LA, Cody Holt threw acting aside.

He held a press conference and announced, no longer did he want anything to do with the cold, phony pretentiousness that formed the covetous world within Hollywood's chosen, inner circle of greed.

For him, that way of life proved only one thing: more is never enough, and never enough, never truly stratifies; only faith in Christ Jesus, he pledged. He even finally revealed his true birth given name, along with a televised invite for the world to watch the symbolic burial of Chaz Spivey, and everything that once represented, Chaz Spivey: scripts, clothes, posters, magazine interviews, SAG card, and numerous awards, which were tossed inside a coffin and slowly lowered into a plot of freshly dug earth. There was also a granite headstone engraved, CHAZ SPIVEY, FOREVER GONE, to ceremonially mark the spot.

Not long after that, Cody Holt left LA, for good, enrolled into a small, but Holy Spirit filled bible college, near Hobbs, New Mexico, graduated with honors, and went on to help Mitch Taylor pastor and guide the congregation at Northside Baptist Church; also presented Luke Aston and Heather Stockton, as husband and wife, to the Lord; but never lost contact with former agent, Derek Harris, his wife, Amber, and of course, precious, little Jessica.

Each phone call in conversation, over the years, always recounted and told how Christ Jesus had showed and saved her and her mommy from the demonically possessed, Tom Nelson, who later spent a lengthy stint behind bars, and also developed strong faith in Christ Jesus, as Savior before being released back into society, where, Tom also said farewell to Hollywood and the music industry, and went back to college and got a degree in education. Tom Nelson now makes a living in Portland, Oregon, as a quiet, mild mannered teacher to high school seniors.

Stories of Curtis Paxton and Ryan Garrett also, still, to this day, fill in-depth conversation between Cody Holt and Jessica, about how they had been there, too, that day, and had arrested Tom Nelson for what he had done.

Of course, nothing truly brings the story to life in true authenticity as how Jessica, now married to Brett Slater, high-power Nashville attorney, took to fleshing it out in words, now published and read by millions.

The novel opens as: These soft, low-grumbling murmurs encapsulated the board meeting at International Creative

Management and swarmed around Derek Harris...*Sound familiar? It should. Now, without doubt, you're probably, more than likely, asking yourself, just who are You?*

I was the One wounded in the house of My friends...And I will carry these nail-scared hands for eternity...Amen.

CONTACT

Lance Garrison welcomes your letters. They should be addressed to:

Lance Garrison
P.O. Box 484
Marlow, OK 73055